Benny and the Giants

and

Other Stories

by

ENID BLYTON

Illustrated by
Ray Mutimer

AWARD PUBLICATIONS LIMITED

For further information on Enid Blyton please contact
www.blyton.com

ISBN 1-84135-208-X

This edition entitled *Benny and the Giants and Other Stories*
published by permission of The Enid Blyton Company

This edition first published 2003
2nd impression 2004

Published by Award Publications Limited,
27 Longford Street, London NW1 3DZ

Printed in Singapore

CONTENTS

Benny
and the Giants

Benny was a little boy with no home, no mother and no father. He went about the world doing odd jobs here and there, earning a penny one day, twopence the next, and maybe nothing the day after.

He was often very lonely. He sometimes looked into windows at night-time when the lamps were lit, and wished he had a cosy home where there was someone who loved him.

"Never mind!" he said to himself. "One day I'll find someone who loves me, and then I can love them back, and we'll have a nice little home together."

One week Benny found it very hard to get work. Nobody seemed to want any jobs done at all. There were no gardens that needed digging, no wood that wanted chopping, and no horses that wanted holding. Benny got very hungry, and wondered whatever he could do. Then he suddenly saw a big notice by the side of the road. This is what it said:

DANGER
BEWARE OF GIANTS

"That's funny," said Benny. "Fancy there being any giants around here!"

He looked round, but he couldn't see any. Then he spied a carter coming slowly towards him, with a load of sacks of potatoes. He hailed him, and asked for a lift.

"You'd better not come with me," said the carter. "I've got to deliver these potatoes a bit too near the giants' castle, for my liking!"

"I'm not afraid!" said Benny. "Let me come, do, for I'm tired."

"Jump up, then," said the carter.

So up Benny sprang, and sat down in the cart. He began to ask the carter

questions about the giants, and the man
told him all he wanted to know.

"There's a giants' castle over yonder,"
he said, pointing with his whip to the
west. "Two great giants live in it, and it
is said that they take people prisoner
when they can, and hold them to ransom.
I heard they were wanting another
servant, but you can guess nobody is
likely to go there!"

"Dear me!" said Benny. "I wonder if

they would take me for their servant. Do you think they would?"

"What! Do you mean to say you'd go to live with great ugly giants?" cried the carter in amazement. "You keep away from them, my boy, or maybe they'll have you for dinner."

Benny thought about it for a little while, and then he made up his mind. He would try to get a job in the giants' castle. That would be better than starving, anyway, and if he thought the giants were likely to eat him he would run away.

"You'd better come back with me on my cart," said the carter, when he had delivered his sacks at a little house by the roadside. "If you get down here, you'll meet the giants, perhaps."

"That's just what I want to do!" said Benny. He leaped down, thanked the surprised carter, and ran down the road. It wound up a hill, and when he came to the top he saw the giants' castle in the distance.

The sun was setting as he came near it,

and the windows glistened and shone.

He walked boldly up to the back door, which was about twenty times as high as he was, and pulled hard at the bell.

The door opened, and a giant servant peered out. He didn't see Benny, who only came about as high as his knee, so

he shut the door again. The boy pulled the bell hard, and once more the giant peered round the door, looking very much surprised.

"Hi!" called Benny. "Look down, not up! Can't you see me?"

The giant looked down in surprise. When he saw Benny he grinned broadly.

"Jumping pigs!" he said. "What a little manikin! What might you want, shrimp?"

"I hear the giants want a servant," said Benny. "Will I do?"

The giant roared with laughter.

"You!" he said. "Why, what could you do?"

"Anything!" said Benny, stepping inside. "Just go and tell the giants I am here, will you?"

The servant gaped at Benny's order, but he turned and trotted off, making a noise like thunder on the wooden floor. Soon he came back again.

"The masters want to see you," he said. So Benny followed him, looking as bold and brave as could be, but inside

he was feeling very trembly indeed.

The two giants who wanted to see him were simply enormous. Their servant seemed quite a dwarf beside them. They picked Benny up, and stood him on a table, looking at him very closely.

"He seems a smart lad," said one of them in a great booming voice.

"He is neat and clean, too," said the other. Then he spoke to Benny.

"We have a little guest with us," he said, with a grin that showed all his big teeth. "She is not eating very well, and we think that our own servant is too clumsy to prepare her meals as she likes them. We want a smaller servant who

11

will please her better. Can you cook, prepare dainty meals, and generally make yourself useful to our guest?"

"Certainly," said Benny, thinking that the giants had a little niece staying with them. "I will do my best."

So the giants engaged him, and he was told to start on his duties the very next day.

Next morning he prepared a nice breakfast, set it on the smallest tray he could find, and then followed the giant servant to the top of the castle. The servant unlocked a heavy door, and flung it open. Benny went in, carrying his tray carefully.

And then he got such a surprise! For the guest was no niece of the giants', but a lovely little princess, who was being kept a prisoner by them. He nearly dropped the tray when he saw her.

"Why!" he cried. "You are no giant! You are a princess! Where do you come from, and how long have you been here?"

"Silence!" shouted the giant servant, cuffing Benny on the ear and nearly

12

stunning him. "The masters say that you and the Princess must not say a word to one another, on pain of death!"

Benny said no more. The Princess said never a word in reply, for she was afraid of getting Benny into trouble. But she managed to give him one or two looks, which told him as plainly as could be that she was unhappy and wanted to escape.

Benny followed the giant servant downstairs, thinking very hard. He thought the little Princess was the loveliest thing he had ever seen. Every time he remembered her sweet face a little warm feeling crept round his heart, so he knew he had fallen in love with her, and he was very happy.

"Now, how can I rescue her?" he wondered. "I must certainly get her away from here!"

"If you think you're going to speak to the Princess, or send messages to her, you can get the idea out of your head!" said the giant servant when they were downstairs again. "I have orders to prevent anything of the sort."

Benny said nothing, for he did not want to anger the servant. Instead, he began to think out delicious meals for the Princess. He made a small tray, and looked for the very tiniest dishes and plates in the castle, for he knew the Princess would not like her meals set on dishes as large as tables.

Then he began to think how he might get her away in safety. First of all, how was he to tell her things? He soon thought of a way. "I'll write my messages on strips of paper," he said. "Then I'll make some cakes, and put the paper round them. Both paper and cake will be baked together, which, as anybody knows, is the right way to bake, and then the Princess can read my messages in secret! Now how can I tell her what I am going to do?"

That night he made himself a bow and a few arrows. He slipped out into the moonlight and looked for the Princess's window. He soon saw it, for she sat by a lamp sewing, and he could see her golden head, bent over her needle.

He wrote a note, and stuck it on the end of an arrow. Then he shot it up at her window. It just missed it, and fell back again. He shot another, with a second note on it. This time he struck the side of the window, and made a noise. The Princess heard it and raised her head.

Benny shot a third arrow. It flew right in at the window, and landed at the feet of the startled maiden. She picked it up, and saw the note.

This is to tell you that I mean to rescue you, she read. *Please tear off the paper you will find round the cakes I bake for you, and you will see my messages written there. Shooting letters with arrows is too dangerous. Take heart, Princess, for I will be your knight.*

Benny.

How glad the Princess was! She ran to the window, and waved her hand in the moonlight. Benny knew that she had read his message, and was content.

Every day he baked her a cake, and wrote his message on the paper round it. The giant servant used to take a

16

skewer and poke it through the cake, to see if Benny had put notes inside – but it never came into his head that the boy had been clever enough to write his messages on the paper baked round the cake itself. So he didn't find out the secret.

Benny tried hard to think of some way of escape. It was very difficult, for the two giants always seemed to be about, and as for the giant servant, he never let Benny out of his sight.

Then, one very hot day, Benny's chance

came. He heard the sound of carriage wheels, and popped his head out of the window. To his joy he saw that the two giants were in the carriage, driving away from the castle.

"That's got rid of two, anyway!" he said. "Now what about the servant? Ah, I've got an idea! If only it will work!

"Where have our masters gone?" he asked the servant. "Will they be long?"

"About six hours," said the giant, with a yawn.

"Then don't let's do any work this afternoon," said Benny. "Let's go to sleep."

"No," said the giant, suspiciously. "You'll run off, if I so much as shut my eyes, I know!"

"Well, I'll do some work, and you just have a nice rest," said Benny. "You'll be able to hear me working, so you'll know I'm here all right. I'll wash and scrub the kitchen floor."

"Very well," said the giant. "I'll put my chair right in the middle, then you don't need to disturb me."

He put his easy chair right in the middle of the vast kitchen and sat down. Benny got out a pail and cloth, and began to wash the floor. He watched the giant carefully, and soon saw that what he hoped would happen, was happening. The giant was falling asleep.

Then Benny ran to the cupboard, and got out the polish, and a duster. He had an idea. He began to polish the wooden floor of the kitchen as if his life depended on it. The giant occasionally opened his eyes, but seeing Benny busy, shut them again at once. The youth went on with

his work, until he had made all the floor shiny and slippery. Then he began to polish the long passage that led out of the kitchen to the hall. The giant heard him, and fell asleep for the sixth time.

When Benny had finished, he crawled on his knees to the snoring giant. He carefully picked the key of the tower-room from the giant's belt and then began to crawl back again. The giant awoke, opened his eyes, and looked for Benny. At once the boy began to rub his duster on the floor, as if he were still cleaning it. The giant shut his eyes, and began to snore once more.

Benny took his chance. He tore up the stairs to the tower-room, unlocked it, and ran to the Princess. He took her hand and begged her to come with him.

"The two giants are out," he said. "As for the servant, he is asleep – but if he awakes and tries to come after us, he will find it difficult to get out of the kitchen for I have polished the floor so highly that he will find it impossible to walk across it!"

The Princess held his hand and together they ran down the stairs. They crept out of the front door, and tiptoed down the steps, afraid of making a noise in case they awakened the giant. But alas! He awoke just at that moment, and heard them!

"Benny!" he called. "Benny! Where are you? Come here at once!"

When no Benny came, the giant leaped to his feet and tried to run across the floor but it was so terribly slippery that he fell on his nose at once! He tried to get up but he couldn't, for the floor was as slippery as ice. He slid here and slipped there, and at last managed to stand up again.

Then *plonk*! Down he went once more. It would have been a funny sight to watch if anyone had been there to see. He scrambled and slipped, and slipped and scrambled, and at last got to the door. But then there was the long slippery passage to go down!

The servant gave it up at last. He was so tired of bumping his nose, his knees and his elbows. He simply sat down on the floor and waited.

Soon the two giants came home. They walked to the kitchen to speak to their servant – and *crash*! Down they both went on the polished floor! They clutched at one another and slid all over the place,

getting mixed up with the surprised servant. At last they all sat still and looked at one another.

"What do you mean by this?" asked the giants, scowling at the servant. "This is a fine thing to do to the floor."

"It's not my fault," said the servant, sulkily. "Benny did it, and now he's gone, and I don't know where he is. He's taken the key of the tower-room too, so I expect the Princess is escaping with him."

"Good gracious!" cried the giants, and tried to leap to their feet. But down they went again, and slithered all along the passage. By the time they managed to get to the front door and start chasing Benny and the Princess it was too late.

Benny was far away. He and the Princess had run for miles. They had passed the notice-board that said "Beware of Giants" and were hurrying to the east. Soon they saw a grand carriage rolling along the road, and Benny sprang out to stop it.

"Ho, ho! What's this!" cried the coachman, flicking at Benny with his

whip. "How dare you stop the carriage of the Lord High Chamberlain?"

"Oh!" squeaked the Princess in delight. "He's my uncle!"

A bearded face appeared at the window, and then the door was flung open.

"Princess! My dear little long-lost niece!" cried the Chamberlain. "How did you come here? We have lost you for months, and looked for you everywhere!"

The Princess hugged him and begged to be taken to her parents, the King and

Queen. Off rolled the carriage once more, with the Chamberlain, the Princess and Benny sitting inside.

It was not long before they arrived at the palace. How glad the King and Queen were to see their little daughter once again! They hugged and kissed her, and shook Benny's hand a hundred times.

"You shall have as much gold as you please, and I will make you a noble lord!" cried the King. "I can never be grateful enough to you."

"And I'll marry you when I'm old enough," the Princess whispered in his ear, "because I love you very much, Benny."

So Benny took his gold and became Sir Benjamin Braveheart. And people do say that next year he is going to marry the Princess, and I shouldn't be at all surprised if it is true!

The Unhappy
Sailor Doll

It was nearly Christmas, and the toys had been asking one another what each of them wanted. "Would you like a new blue bow, Teddy?" said Angela the doll.

"How about some of your favourite iced buns?" the pink cat asked the toy dog.

"Would you like a little tiny knocker for the front door of your ark?" the sailor doll asked Noah. He was very good at carving things out of wood, and he felt sure he could make a fine knocker.

But nobody asked the sailor doll what he would like. He knew what he wanted – a new blue bow for his jacket, new laces for his shoes, and a little pin for his hat.

"And nobody has asked me once what I'd like!" thought the sailor doll, gloomily.

"It's too bad. Don't they like me? I know what I'll do. I'll ask Clockwork Mouse what he would like – and he is sure to say, 'And now, Sailor, tell me what you would like'!"

So the sailor doll asked the mouse – but all he said was, "Oh, please, I'd like two new whiskers!" He didn't ask the sailor doll what he wanted.

"That proves it!" said the sailor doll, miserably. "They don't like me. They're not going to give me any presents. Yet they've all told me what they want. Well, I'll give them the presents they want but I shall run away just before Christmas! That will make them very, very sorry."

The toys couldn't think why Sailor Doll looked so gloomy.

They got a bit tired of his miserable face after a while, and took no notice of him. That made him feel worse than ever!

Just before Christmas the sailor doll decided it was time to run away. "They'll be glad to have Christmas without me!"

he thought. "Now – I want a little bag to pack my things in. Where is there one?"

He remembered seeing a little suitcase in the toy cupboard. He found it at last and took it over to a corner to pack his few things in it.

"It feels a bit heavy," said Sailor Doll, surprised. "I hope there's nothing in it."

He opened it – and out tumbled a whole lot of tiny parcels, all done up in bits of Christmassy paper and tied with pretty string. Each one had a label. Sailor read them, and his cheeks blushed pink. *To Sailor with love, For dear Sailor from*

the Clockwork Mouse, For the nicest Sailor Doll in the world from Angela.

Sailor Doll put everything back quickly into the little suitcase. Why – these were all presents hidden away by the toys, that they were going to give him at Christmas!

"I'm so ashamed of myself," he said. "To think I got this suitcase to run away with – and it's the one the toys have hidden all the lovely presents in that they've made me for Christmas. I'm bad.

I'm mean! I don't deserve any presents at all!"

He put the suitcase back. He felt so happy. The toys liked him after all! He was their "dear Sailor". Fancy that! Well, it just showed how silly it was to think people didn't like you. He worked hard at his presents for the others, making them as nicely as he could. He joked and smiled and was so very different that all the toys were surprised.

"He's a real dear," they said. "What a good thing we've got all the things he wants for Christmas. We didn't need to ask him, because we knew. How he'll love his new blue bow and hat pin and shoelaces and everything!"

He will, of course – but he shivers when he remembers how he nearly ran away!

The Pixie Who Killed the Moon

Once upon a time there was a silly little pixie called Big Eyes. He never stopped to think about anything at all, and he always believed every single thing he was told.

When a chestnut fell down on his head one night he ran away in terror, shouting at the top of his voice: "A star has fallen on me! A star has fallen on me!"

The other pixies, who had seen the chestnut fall, laughed at him. "Catch it, then!" they cried. "It is shining in your hair!"

Big Eyes leaned over a pool and, sure enough, he saw a star shining, as he thought, in his hair.

He took a comb and combed all night, but he couldn't find the star. I'm not surprised, either. Are you?

Another time he heard a nightingale singing and he wanted to take it home to live with him, but it wouldn't come. It sat in its bush and sang beautifully, and took no notice of Big Eyes.

"Build a fence round the bush!" said the other pixies. "Then he can't get away, Big Eyes."

So Big Eyes gathered a great deal of pieces of wood and made a tight little fence all round the bush.

The nightingale watched him with great interest. "What's that for, Big Eyes?" he asked.

"Wait and see," said Big Eyes.

So the nightingale waited. When the fence was finished Big Eyes jumped over it and laughed.

"Ho! ho!" he cried. "Now I've got you, my little nightingale! Come home with me and live in my cottage. You shall have wild strawberries for breakfast, and I will polish your beak every morning for you."

"No, not I," said the nightingale.

"But you must," said Big Eyes.

"Trilla – trilla – trilla!" sang the nightingale mockingly. "You cannot make me!"

"Yes, I can!" said Big Eyes. "I have built a fence all around you, and you cannot escape me. I shall catch you and take you home with me."

"Catch me, then!" cried the nightingale, and spread his wings. He flew straight up and over the fence and disappeared, singing, into the wood.

All the pixies laughed as Big Eyes stared in dismay.

"Why don't you think, Big Eyes?" they cried. "You knew that a nightingale could fly! Why didn't you think?"

Big Eyes was upset but he didn't try to mend his ways – not he! It was too much bother, and he wasn't going to try.

Now one day a child went through the wood in which Big Eyes lived. She carried a big yellow balloon, and it floated prettily behind her. Suddenly there came a great gust of wind and – *puff*! – the string was blown out of her hand and the balloon went sailing away into the wood. It floated through the air for a long time, until it came to the place where Big Eyes was having his dinner.

It landed just by him and stayed there with its string caught in a bramble bush.

Big Eyes jumped up in fright, for he had heard no noise and hadn't seen the balloon coming.

Crash! went his bowl; and *splash!* went his soup, while Big Eyes fled through the wood, howling with fright.

"What's the matter?" cried everyone.

"The moon's fallen down by me," wept Big Eyes, "the big yellow moon! It came while I was eating my dinner, and almost killed me!"

The pixies laughed loudly and went to see what it was.

"Isn't he silly?" they said, when they saw it was only a balloon. "He always cries before he's hurt. Let's pretend it *is* the moon, and see what he'll do!"

So they pretended it was the moon, and Big Eyes told them again and again how it had nearly fallen on his head and killed him.

"It was a shame to give you such a fright!" said the pixies. "I should punish the moon if I were you!"

"How?" asked Big Eyes.

"Well, prick it with a pin!" said the

pixies. "That will make the moon squeal out and punish it severely. But wait until it's asleep in the hot sun!"

So Big Eyes waited. Next day he got a very long pin and hid himself in the bushes near by. Then, when the sun was high in the sky at midday and he thought the moon was sleeping, he crept up to it.

With a trembling hand he stuck the pin into the fat yellow balloon.

BANG! It burst with a tremendous explosion, and Big Eyes was nearly frightened to death. All the watching

pixies were, too, and tumbled head over heels in the bushes.

Big Eyes fled for his life. He jumped down a rabbit-hole and sat there trembling.

"Oh dear! Oh dear!" he said. "I've killed the moon! It's burst all to nothing! I've killed the moon. What will the Fairy Queen say to me? Oh dear! Oh dear, dear!"

The more he thought about it the more he shivered and shook.

"I've killed it dead!" he said. "Bang! it went, like that – and all because I pricked it with a pin! How was I to know that would kill the moon? And now we won't be able to dance in the moonlight any more!"

All that day and all that night, and the next day too, Big Eyes sat in his hole, sad and sorry.

"I didn't mean to," he wept. "It was only to punish the moon for frightening me. I hope the Queen won't be angry!"

When the evening of the next day came poor Big Eyes determined to go to the

Queen and confess what he had done.

So he crept out of his hole and made his way to the glade where the Fairy Queen held her court. She was there, and welcomed the trembling little pixie.

"Oh, Your Majesty!" wept Big Eyes. "I've done a dreadful thing! I've killed the moon!"

"Killed the moon!" said the Queen in astonishment. "You can't have done that, Big Eyes!"

"But I did!" said Big Eyes. "I pricked it with a pin and it went bang! – like that, and died!"

The Fairy Queen laughed. Then she took Big Eyes by the arm and pointed to a hill in the distance.

"See!" she said. "What is that peeping over the hill yonder?"

Big Eyes looked. It was the big round moon, yellow and bright, rising slowly above the hill.

He stared in astonishment. So he hadn't killed it, after all.

"The other pixies have made fun of you instead of helping you!" said the Queen. "They will be punished. And you, Big Eyes, you must use your brains and think. Go back to the pixie school and learn all you can. Then you will never be so silly again!"

Big Eyes was so glad to think that he hadn't really killed the moon that he went home singing all the way. And I'm sure you will be glad to know that he was never so stupid again!

The Moon in the Pail

One night the moon was full. It hung in the sky like a great white globe, and shone marvellously.

"I wonder who hung that lamp in the sky tonight," said Bobs, the black-and-white fox terrier. "It's lighting up the whole garden. It's wonderful. I like it."

"Do you see how it sails in and out of the clouds?" said Cosy, the tabby cat. "I'd like to do that. It would be fun."

"I wish I had the moon for my own," said Topsy, the fox terrier puppy. "I would like such a lovely thing to play with. I would roll it down the garden path, and it would give me light wherever it went. Oh, I do wish I had it."

"I'll get it for you," said Bimbo, the naughty Siamese kitten, grinning. "What will you give me if I do?"

"I'll give you the big bone that the butcher-boy threw to me this morning," said Topsy, after she had thought for a while. "That's what I'll give you. I've hidden it away and nobody knows where it is. But I'll give it to you if you really will get me the moon to play with."

"Right!" said Bimbo, and ran off. He came to where the cook had stood an empty pail outside the kitchen door. He dragged it to the garden tap and filled the pail full of water.

The reflection of the bright moon shone in the pail of water. It looked lovely there, round and bright, just like the moon in the sky.

Bimbo waited until the water was quite still, and the moon shone there, round and beautiful. Then he ran off to find Topsy.

"Topsy!" he mewed. "I've got the moon for you. Come and see."

"Oh, where!" cried Topsy in delight, and ran off with Bimbo to the pail.

"Look in my pail of water," said Bimbo.

42

"Do you see the moon there? Well, you can have it."

"Yes, it's really there," said Topsy, looking at the reflection of the bright moon there. It really did look exactly as if the moon had fallen into the pail! "Oh, Bimbo, how good and clever you are to get me the moon, as I asked. But why did you put it into a pail of water?"

"Well, it might have got out if it hadn't got water over it," said Bimbo at once. "Now, Topsy, remember your promise – where's that big bone you hid away?"

"I'll show you," said Topsy, and she took Bimbo to where the yew hedge grew. She dug about a little and sniffed. Then she began to scrabble and scrape for all she was worth, and at last, up came the great big juicy bone that the butcher-boy had given to Topsy. It was rather dirty, but Bimbo didn't mind that! He took it in his mouth and ran off.

"You go and play with your moon!" said Bimbo, with a laugh. So off Topsy went to the pail of water.

The moon still swam there, round and bright. Topsy sat down and looked into the water. "Come on out, Moon," she said. "I want to play with you. Come out, and I will roll you down the path like a big shining ball, and every little mouse and hedgehog, every beetle and worm, will come out to watch you rolling by!"

But the moon didn't come out. It stayed in the pail and shone there, silvery bright.

"Do come out!" begged Topsy. "Please do. It must be so nasty and cold there in the water, and so wet, too. That's the horrid thing about water, it's always so wet. If it was dry, it would be much nicer to bathe in."

The moon shone there, but it didn't come out. Topsy grew angry.

"Do you want me to put my nose into the water and get you out?" she barked. "You won't like that. I might nip you with my teeth, Moon. Come along out, do!"

But the moon didn't. Topsy sat and looked at it, with her head on one side. "Well, I shall put in my nose, then," she said. "And I shall get hold of you. So look out!"

She put her nose into the water and tried to get hold of the moon. But, of course, the moon wasn't really there, so all that poor Topsy got was a mouthful of water that made her choke and cough. She was very angry.

"Do you know what I am going to do?" she wuffed. "I am going to tip the pail over, then the water will run out and away, and you will find yourself on the ground for me to play with!"

So Topsy tipped over the pail, and out went the water with a gurgling noise all over the ground. Topsy waited to jump on

the moon, but what a peculiar thing, no moon came out of the pail!

"Where's it gone, where's it gone?" howled Topsy, scraping about the ground as if she thought the moon was stuck there. "She was in the water, and the water's out, but the moon isn't."

"Whatever is the matter?" said Bobs, wandering up. "What are you doing dancing round that empty pail, Topsy? Have you suddenly gone mad?"

"No," said Topsy. "But a very sad thing has happened, Bobs. Bimbo got the moon and put her into a pail of water for me. I tipped up the pail to get the moon out, but somehow she's slipped away and gone. I can't find her."

"Well, I know where she's gone," said Bobs, with a sudden giggle.

"Where?" said Topsy, in surprise.

"Back to the sky. Look!" said Bobs. And when Topsy looked up into the sky, sure enough there was the bright round moon sailing along between the clouds as quickly as ever!

"Well! To think she jumped back there

so quickly!" said Topsy, in surprise. "Bimbo! Bimbo! Give me back my bone! The moon's got out of the pail and has gone back to the sky!"

But Bimbo was nowhere to be found. Neither was the bone! I'm not at all surprised, are you?

They Ran
Away

"Let's run away!" said Bill. "I'm fed up with the farm."

"So am I," said Ben. "Who'd live on a farm if they could live in a city?"

"Cinemas every night!" said Bill.

"Buses, trains, trams, people, everywhere noise and lights and something going on. How exciting!" said Ben.

"Nothing ever goes on at a farm," said Bill. "It's a dead boring place. Nothing to do. No one to talk to. Nowhere to go. Come on – let's go now!"

So off they went, that bright spring morning. They caught the bus, and they got to the city in two hours time. It was exciting! The noise, the traffic, the shops, the people. My, this was life!

They went for rides on buses. They

went walking in the crowded streets, and got pushed here and there. They went to two cinemas, and then found that they were so tired they could do nothing else but go to bed. They found a woman who let them have a hot, stuffy, smelly little room for the night.

But they couldn't go to sleep.

"I do miss my dog Rusty," said Bill. "He'll be wondering where I am."

"And my dog Scamp will be howling for me," said Ben.

"I reckon old Buttercup and Daisy, the

cows we milk, will wonder where we are," said Bill.

"And Captain and Blossom, the horses – do you suppose they're all right?" said Ben.

"Those little lambs we've fed with the bottle," said Bill. "I keep on thinking of them. Growing into frisky little things they are."

"I hope Pa's shut the hens in all right," said Ben. "That fox is about again, you know. I shouldn't want him to get those little chicks."

"Or the ducklings either," said Bill.

"I guess that field of corn's going to come along well this weather," said Ben.

"What do we care about that?" said Bill. "We won't be there to see it. We'll be here."

They lay still for a few minutes. Then Ben suddenly threw off the covers. "I want my dog Scamp," he said. "I shouldn't have left him behind."

"Well, I want my dog Rusty, too," said Bill. "Come on – we'll go back and get them."

So back they went, walking mile after mile in the moonlight. At last they came to the farm. They stood at the gate of the Long Field.

"Corn's grown a bit today, I do declare," said Ben.

A bleating came to their ears and up ran three well-grown lambs. They butted their heads against the boys' legs. "Why, it's our bottle-fed lambs!" said Bill. "Frisky, Scamper and Wriggle."

"Moo-oo!" said a voice, and Buttercup the cow looked over the hedge. Daisy looked over, too. Ben reached up and rubbed their noses. "Are you glad to see us back? My, you should just see the city, Buttercup!"

There was a thudding of big hooves. That was Captain, the great shire horse. He neighed. Ben got up on the gate nearby and hugged the big brown head to him.

"Captain! Who groomed you tonight? Did you miss me?" asked Ben. "Hello, Blossom. Bill, here's Blossom looking for you."

The boys fondled the horses and then
went quietly through the moonlit
farmyard. They peeped into the hen-
house, they looked at the ducklings
cuddled with their foster mothers in a
coop or two. They stroked Ribby, the
stable cat, and asked how her kittens
were.

And then there came such a barking
that they were nearly deafened! It was
Rusty and Scamp locked up in the stables
nearby. They scraped excitedly at the
door, and went quite mad with joy at
hearing their young masters' voices
again.

Ben opened the door. The two dogs flung themselves on them, whining and yelping. They licked every bit of bare skin they could find, hands, faces, necks, ears.

"Oh, Rusty! I'll never leave you behind again!" said Bill.

"And I'm going to take Scamp with me wherever I go!" said Ben, hugging his dog. "How could I have gone without him?"

"Better start back again," said Bill, after a bit. "Have to be gone before Pa gets up in the morning."

"I'm tired," said Ben. "I guess I'll go and have a bit of a snooze in the barn before I start back."

"So will I," said Bill. "Come on, Rusty – you can cuddle up to me."

In two minutes all four were sound asleep, and they didn't wake till the sun was streaming in through the door of the barn.

"My word – there's Buttercup mooing," said Bill, sleepily. "She wants to be milked. I'll do the cows this morning, Ben – you see to the hens, and bring the horses in if Pa wants them."

"Lovely morning!" said Ben. "Nice and noisy, too, Bill – hear the hens clucking, and the ducks quacking and old Buttercup mooing, and the dogs barking, and the lark up there singing like mad."

"Yes. Seems to me there's more creatures about here than there are people in a city," said Bill. "And lots more to do – and sunshine and wind to do it in. Reckon I'd rather be too busy down in the country, Ben, than not have much to do in a city."

"Better to be like Pa – wear out and not rust out," said Ben. "Well, what about this running away, Bill?"

"What running away?" said Bill. "Well – I've run away to the city and now I've run back to the country, and I just feel I don't want to do any more running for a very long time."

"Funny. I feel the same," said Ben. "Hey Scamp, come along – there's work to do down here on the farm. Hey, Pa! You let those horses be! They're my job!"

Billy's
Bicycle

Billy had a bicycle. It had belonged to his brother, and when John had grown too big for it he had put it into the shed and left it there all by itself. John had had a new one, and so the old bicycle had lain there, rusty and forgotten.

When Billy grew big enough for a bicycle he remembered John's. "Oh, I wonder if it would do for me, or if it is too broken and old!" he thought.

So he went to have a look at it. There it was in the shed, leaning against the seed-boxes and the barrel of oil.

Billy looked at it. "I like the look of you," he said to the bicycle. "You certainly look old, but you look nice and friendly somehow – as if you'd like me to ride on you."

Now this was just exactly what the bicycle was feeling! It badly wanted Billy to ride it. It liked the look of him very much, for Billy was one of those smiley children that everyone likes.

Billy took the bicycle out into the garden. "My goodness, you are rusty!" he said. "Your paint is all worn off and your bell is broken – it won't ring. I don't think much of you at the moment, but I do believe I could make you quite smart again if I get a pot of paint, and if I rub the rust off your bright parts."

The bicycle was thrilled to hear this. It is dreadful to be old, rusty and dirty – and simply lovely to hear somebody say that they can make you look fine again. The bicycle wished it had a bell to ring. It felt quite sure it would have rung it for joy, if it had!

Well, Billy was as good as his word. He spent some money on a pot of black paint and a pot of red paint. He painted that bicycle till it looked as new as could be. He rubbed away the rust, and made the bright parts shine.

58

"I'll buy a new bell for you and a new saddlebag," said Billy. "I'll have your brakes put right too. And there's a screw gone at the back. I'll get that put right. And I'll pump up your tyres and ride you! You and I will have some fine times together, bike!"

Well, in a week's time that bicycle was just like a new one. It shone beautifully, and its new bell rang as loudly as could be! Its tyres were nice and hard, and spun along the road joyfully.

The old bicycle was very happy. It loved to feel Billy on its saddle, pedalling away hard. It helped him all it could. It tried not to run over big stones. It tried not to go into puddles and splash him.

They had some good times together, Billy and the bike. They went everywhere – to school, to the park, to the hills, and to the woods. The bicycle enjoyed itself tremendously. It had been so lonely and sad lying in the dark shed by itself.

Now it could talk to other bicycles and cars and could have its bell rung at corners so that it felt most important! Ah, this was the kind of life for a bicycle!

Billy kept his bicycle beautifully. He cleaned it well. He kept the bright parts shining. He oiled it and pumped up the tyres properly. He didn't fling it down on the ground as other boys did with their bicycles. And the old bike loved him for it, and sang a little purring song as it went along the road.

"I wish I could do something for Billy!" it sang. "Billy's done plenty for me! I wish I could do something for Billy!

Billy's done plenty for me!"

Now one evening, when the bicycle was leaning against the shed, waiting for Billy to come out and put it away, it was surprised to see a boy's head peeping just over the fence.

"What's that boy doing?" thought the bicycle in surprise. "Why is he peeping all round like that? This is very strange."

The boy saw that nobody was about. He jumped over the fence and ran to the apple-shed in which were stored all the cooking and eating apples. My word, that

boy was going to have a feast!

The bicycle watched him go into the apple-shed. He heard him munching apples. He saw him filling a sack with them. And the bicycle was very angry!

"Billy's mother may think that Billy took those apples!" it said. It wondered what to do. It couldn't ride off by itself and warn Billy. But it could ring its bell!

So it rang it. *R-r-r-r-ring, r-r-r-r-ring, r-r-r-r-ring! R-r-r-ring!*

The boy in the shed was alarmed. He put his head out to see what was happening. He didn't for one moment think that it was the bicycle bell ringing!

But he saw the bicycle and an idea came into his head. He could ride it away quickly and nobody would catch him!

He put the sack of apples over his shoulder, ran to the bicycle, jumped on it and rode it away. The bicycle rang its bell in despair:

R-r-r-ring! R-r-r-ring! R-r-r-ring!

But Billy was out with his father and couldn't hear it. So out of the gate the bike had to go, with the bad boy riding it.

How it hated it! But it couldn't help itself, for when its pedals were pushed round and round it just had to go!

And then, coming down the street, the bicycle saw Billy and his father! They were going home. The bicycle was so excited. Now perhaps Billy would see it!

But Billy was looking into the shops as he passed and he didn't notice his bicycle. So the bicycle rang its bell desperately again:

R-r-r-ring! R-r-r-ring! R-r-r-ring!

Billy looked round. He knew the sound of that bicycle bell. He stared hard at the bicycle as it went by. Could it possibly be his? No – surely it couldn't!

The bicycle saw a big stone in its way. It ran at it, and wobbled over it. The bad boy tried to balance himself, but he couldn't, because the bicycle wobbled so. Down he fell with a crash and the apples flew all over the road!

Billy and his father went to help him up. The bicycle rang its bell again:

R-r-r-ring! R-r-r-ring! R-r-r-ring!

Then Billy looked closely at the bicycle

and he knew that it was his. What an extraordinary thing!

"What are you doing on my bicycle?" he asked the boy. "You bad boy – and I think those are our apples too!"

The boy began to cry. He had hurt his knee very badly, and he was frightened, for he knew that he had done very wrong. He confessed all that he had done, and Billy's father looked very stern.

"You will come back to our house and I will bind up your knee," he said. "Then I shall take you back to your own home and speak to your father about you. I think you need to have a good punishment, and I shall see that you get it. How dare you come to my apple-shed, steal my apples, and ride off on my son's bicycle! It's a good thing you rang the bell when you did, or Billy wouldn't have heard it and looked round."

"I didn't ring the bell," said the boy, wiping his eyes with a very dirty hand. "It seemed to ring all by itself. It was very strange."

"Bells don't ring by themselves," said Billy's father. But he was wrong, wasn't he! And just to show that he was, the bicycle rang its bell again, very softly and happily:

R-r-r-ring! R-r-r-ring! R-r-r-r-ring! I've done something for Billy at last! R-r-r-ring! R-r-r-ring! R-r-r-r-ring!

She Didn't Want to Go to School

Marigold was very small, only five years old. She was so shy that she could never even say "Quite well, thank you," when people said to her, "How are you, little Marigold?"

And now her mother said she must go to school. Marigold was frightened. School! She would never be able to answer a single question. She would have to do all kinds of hard and difficult things. She would have to read books, and she didn't know how to.

"Well, you will learn," said her mother.

"But I don't even know how to learn," said Marigold, and burst into tears.

"Oh, dear – if you behave like that your teacher will certainly be cross with you," said Mother, and that made poor

Marigold feel even worse. She couldn't bear people to be cross with her.

"You can go with the big children next door, when school begins next Tuesday," said Mother.

Marigold didn't like the idea of that at all. She was afraid of the big children. Why, Laurie was ten! He seemed almost grown-up to Marigold. She never dared to speak a word to him.

She thought and thought about school. She wouldn't go! She would run away from the big children, and they wouldn't be able to find her. She would hide somewhere till dinner-time came and she could go home.

Wasn't she a silly little girl? But she was only five, and she had never been to school before.

"Marigold, you musn't look so worried about school," said Mother that night. "You will perhaps find a nice little friend of your own there. You haven't any real friends since your cousins left our town."

"I don't want a friend," said Marigold, sulkily. "I'm happy by myself. I want to stay at home for always and always, and never go the school."

"Now you're just being silly," said Mother.

Well, Tuesday morning came, and Mother got Marigold ready. She had a nice new school-bag with two new pencils, a rubber, some crayons and a ruler in it. She had a new school hat and a school blazer, blue with a red pocket. But she didn't like any of these nice new things at all – they meant school.

"There go the big children from next door. Go and join them," said Mother,

kissing Marigold goodbye. "Your teacher is expecting you, because I saw her last week. Hurry along now – you'll have a lovely time."

Marigold went out of the house and joined the other children. Only Laurie took any notice of her.

"Hello!" he said. "Going to school for the first time? Tag along with us then."

But Marigold only went with them for a little way. When she got to the next corner she ran round it and left the other children to go straight on down the street.

She was running away! She wouldn't go to school, she just wouldn't. Nobody could make her. But where could she hide away that morning?

She felt very lonely and frightened. She began to cry as she went down the road and round another corner. She didn't see a big girl and a little girl coming along and she bumped into them.

"Oh, I say – did I hurt you?" said the big girl. "I've made you cry! Poor little thing! Did I bump you?"

Marigold didn't like to say she had been crying before she had bumped into them. "Where are you going?" she asked. "I'm nearly lost."

"Are you? Well, come with us then," said the big girl. "Look, this is my little sister, Mary-Jane. Take her hand. She's rather shy, so she won't say much to you – but she's very, very nice."

The two little girls looked at one another. "I'm going to play a drum this morning," said Mary-Jane, suddenly. "And I'm going to jump about like a frog."

71

This sounded exciting. Marigold liked beating drums, too, and she was very good at leaping about like a frog.

"Can I come with you?" she said. "I should like to play a drum."

"Yes, of course you can come," said the big girl. "You'll be company for my shy little sister."

So Marigold trotted along with Mary-Jane and her big sister, Lulu. They came to a side entrance to a big house and went in. Lulu took Mary-Jane to a door where a lot of other little children were gathering into a line. A smiling-faced woman was talking to them.

"Miss Thomas, this is my little sister Mary-Jane," said Lulu. "And we picked up this little girl on the way. She's called Marigold."

"Oh yes – Marigold Peters," said Miss Thomas, and she smiled at Marigold. "Would you and Mary-Jane like to have these two pegs next to one another to put your hats on? That's right. What a beautiful school-bag, Marigold!"

Marigold was pleased to hear her

school-bag called beautiful. She opened it and showed Miss Thomas all the things inside it.

"What nice crayons!" said Miss Thomas. "Can you crayon nicely? I wish you would crayon me a picture this morning."

"Mary-Jane says she's going to play a drum," said Marigold.

"Oh, yes. You can too, if you like," said Miss Thomas. "We've got six drums – look, here they are. Aren't they beauties?"

They certainly were! They were very big and had a pair of sticks each.

Marigold longed to beat one. She thought this was a very nice place indeed. The big girl Lulu had now disappeared, but little Mary-Jane was still there. Marigold kept close to her. She liked her very much.

Well, Marigold had a perfectly lovely morning. She marched in a line with the others while Miss Thomas played the piano. She banged the drum. She crayoned three lovely pictures. She sang all the nursery rhymes she knew, and was very pleased when Miss Thomas said she knew more than anyone else.

At eleven o'clock all the small children went out to play together in the garden. Mary-Jane and Marigold kept together, and although they were both shy they liked hide-and-seek so much that they couldn't help playing it with the others.

Afterwards Miss Thomas told them a story. Marigold loved stories. "Do you often tell stories to the children?" she asked Miss Thomas at the end. Nobody could possibly be shy with Miss Thomas. She was so nice.

"Oh, yes – I tell stories every day," said Miss Thomas. "I know hundreds."

Marigold thought about that. This was a nice place to come to. Mary-Jane was lucky to come here each day. Marigold wished she could too. Why couldn't she come here instead of going to that frightening place, school? She made up her mind to tell her mother that she had run away that morning from the big children, and had found this lovely place.

When she and Mary-Jane ran out of the door at half past twelve, what a surprise Marigold got! Her mother was there, waiting for her! But however did she know that Marigold was there? The little girl rushed up to her.

"Mummy, how did you know I was here? Oh, Mummy, can I come here every morning with Mary-Jane! It's such a lovely place, much, much better than school! I banged a drum and sang and

marched and crayoned some pictures. Mummy, do say I can come again!"

"But darling – what do you mean?" said her mother. "This *is* your school! This is where you were meant to go. That's why I came here to fetch you this morning. It's your own school!"

Well! What do you think of that? Marigold could hardly believe her ears. She went very red and looked up at her mother.

"I've been silly," she said. "I thought I wouldn't go to school. I thought I'd run away and hide this morning. And then I thought I would go with Mary-Jane and bang a drum. But I didn't guess it was school. Oh, Mummy – it's a lovely place! I don't ever want to miss a single day."

Marigold is still at the same school. She goes with Mary-Jane each day and they are firm friends. They are eight years old now, and it was Marigold who told me about that very first day. I really thought I must tell the story to you!

Klip-Klap and the Fireworks

Klip-Klap was a most meddlesome little gnome. He couldn't keep his nose or his fingers out of anything. The people in his village got so cross with him but it wasn't a bit of use, he still went on poking his nose into everybody else's business.

When Mother Wump baked her cakes one day, he smelled the lovely smell of them, and went to see what was being baked.

"You go away," said Mother Wump, waving her rolling-pin at him. "You're a meddlesome creature, you are, Klip-Klap, and I don't want to see you in my kitchen."

But Klip-Klap begged to stay, and said that he would watch the cakes carefully, so that Mother Wump could get on with her bed-making. So she left him by the oven, and went to her bedroom.

But that stupid little gnome kept opening the oven-door every minute to see if the cakes were done and, of course, as everyone knows, that spoils cakes at once. Then he took them out and dug his finger into them to see if they were going to be nice and crisp. That didn't do them any good either. But when he bit round the edges to see if they tasted nice, that made them look simply dreadful!

Mother Wump was cross. She boxed his ears and sent him howling out of her kitchen.

"You naughty little thing!" she cried, in a fine rage. "You've spoilt my cakes with your prodding and nibbling! Be off with you, or I'll complain to Quick-Eye."

Quick-Eye was the chief of the village, and he punished anyone who needed it. So Klip-Klap was frightened, and scampered away as fast as he could.

The next thing he poked his nose into was little Silver-Toes' dressmaking. She was trying hard to make herself a nice new party dress, and getting on very well indeed when Klip-Klap put his head round the door and asked her what she was doing.

"You go away," she said. "I don't want you interfering here, Klip-Klap."

"Oh, do let me see what you are doing," said the gnome, and ran over to her. "Why, you're not doing this right, Silver-Toes! This piece of cloth should be that way, and that piece this way! And those buttons ought to go there, not here."

Silver-Toes thought the gnome knew what he was talking about – but he didn't. She let him tell her this and that – and, oh dear, when the dress was finished, what a sight it was! It was all back to front, and there was one sleeve long and one sleeve short. The buttons were at the bottom instead of the top, so you can guess it looked terrible.

Silver-Toes was so upset. She sobbed and cried and went to tell Quick-Eye how Klip-Klap had spoiled her dress through his meddling.

"The very next time that gnome pokes his nose into other folk's business, I'll turn him out of the village," said Quick-Eye, sternly. "He shall be sent to the world of boys and girls, and he'll soon be taught a lesson if he starts meddling there."

Well, it wasn't long before Klip-Klap fell into disgrace again, as you can imagine. He went to help Quick-Eye's cook with her washing-up, and when he saw her making a fine apple-pie he longed to meddle with it.

"She hasn't put enough sugar in it, I'm sure," he thought to himself, looking at the apples as they lay all neatly sliced in the pie-dish. "I'll put in some more. Then Quick-Eye will say how nice and sweet it is."

He got a tin and emptied some of the white stuff in it over the apples. He didn't bother to look at the label, or he would have seen it said SALT on it, not SUGAR. The cook didn't notice what he was doing – she was busy rolling out the pastry.

When the pie was cooked, and Quick-

Eye cut some for his dinner, he put a very large spoonful into his mouth, for he was fond of apple-pie. He swallowed it hurriedly, for it tasted horrible.

"Dear me, now was that my imagination, or did it really taste like that?" he wondered. "It must have been my imagination. Apple-pies taste lovely."

So he took another mouthful, but oh dear, it tasted worse than the other. Quick-Eye spluttered and choked, and then rang the bell furiously for the cook.

"It must have been that naughty little Klip-Klap meddling as usual," said the cook. "I'll call him."

They soon found out what the gnome had done. "I meant to make the pie sweet," he said sulkily. "I didn't know that tin had salt in. It looked just like sugar."

"Well, this is the end of your meddling in this village," said Quick-Eye, angrily. "You are not a bit sorry for what you have done, I can see. Go away from here at once, and take the bus to the world of boys and girls. I am sure you will learn such a sharp lesson there that you will soon be cured of your bad habit."

"I shall love to go away to the boys and girls!" said Klip-Klap rudely, and ran off to catch the bus. He was just in time to get a seat by the driver. Off they went over the hills and through the fields. It wasn't long before they came to the little village in our world that lies just on the borders of Fairyland.

Klip-Klap got off the bus, and ran happily along the road. He didn't care a

bit about his punishment! He was excited
to think he was in a strange land.

Now it so happened that it was
November the Fifth, Guy Fawkes Day,
when he arrived. All the boys and girls
were busy buying fireworks for the
evening time. One boy, Peter Penny, had
bought such a lot – rockets, Catherine
wheels, jumping squibs, Roman candles,
golden rain, and many others.

Klip-Klap met him as he was coming
out of the shop, and stared at all the
fireworks he was carrying.

"What are those?" he asked.

"Well, fancy not knowing what fireworks are!" cried Peter Penny, in surprise. "Where do you come from that you don't know that?"

"I come from the Village of Gnomes, in Fairyland," said Klip-Klap. "I'm on a visit here. What do those fireworks do?"

"Come home with me and I'll show you," said Peter Penny. So the gnome trotted along with the boy. Peter Penny wasn't very big, but the gnome was much smaller than he was, and they looked very funny going along together, hoppitty-skip, skippitty-hop.

At last they came to Peter Penny's house, and ran in at the back gate. Peter put down the fireworks in the back garden, and Klip-Klap looked at them inquisitively.

"What do you do with them?" he asked.

"You must wait until seven o'clock tonight, and then you'll see," said Peter Penny. "Look, this is a rocket, and this is a Catherine wheel."

"What do they do?" asked Klip-Klap,

turning them over in his hands.

"Ha ha!" said Peter. "Wait and see. You want a few matches, little gnome, before the fireworks do anything! Look, come and help me to put them in this shed, ready for tonight. Then if you would like to stay here and look after them for me, you can come to my firework party this evening. Be sure not to meddle with them though."

Klip-Klap helped Peter Penny to put the fireworks into a tiny shed. Then he went in himself, and Peter shut the door. Klip-Klap meant to look after them till the evening came.

But the gnome soon grew tired of waiting.

"I wonder if these fireworks really are exciting," he said. "I think I'll light one and find out. I've got a box of matches in my pocket, I know."

He took them out and struck a match. By its light he saw a squib. He held a match to it, and waited to see what would happen.

Well, you can guess what happened. The squib, as soon as it was properly alight, began to jump about! Klip-Klap hadn't expected that! Dear me no! He was terribly frightened. The squib leaped right off the little shelf and jumped at the gnome. Klip-Klap gave a scream and tried to get out of its way, but the shed was so small that he couldn't.

The squib landed on his right arm, and burned a hole in his sleeve. Then it

jumped on his foot, and back to the shelf
again. It landed on a Catherine wheel
and lit it.

Z-z-z-z-z! Splutter! Bang! The Catherine wheel went off too. It jumped about
on the shelf, and Klip-Klap watched it
in terror. He tried to stop it from leaping
off the shelf, but he took hold of it just as
it was going to go round and round and
round and the little gnome found himself being whirled round with it. How
frightened he was!

Soon the squib set light to the other
fireworks too. A Prince of Wales feather
suddenly sent out a stream of golden
stars and feathers over the terrified

gnome. They didn't burn him, of course, but he thought they were going to, for he had never seen fireworks before. He jumped this way and that, and then found another jumping squib was alight.

That was a very mischievous squib. It seemed to know that Klip-Klap was frightened of it, for it leaped out at him in a very sudden manner from this corner and that. The gnome shouted in fright, and trod on a box of coloured matches. In a moment they flared up too, and the little shed was lit up with green, blue, red and yellow flares.

It was really dreadful to be shut up in a tiny place with so many exploding fireworks. How Klip-Klap wished that he had never left his gnome village! How he wished he had never meddled with anything all his life long!

But the worst was still to come. The Catherine wheel set light to a whole heap of rockets, and they began to explode one after another.

Zip! Bang! Crash! Wallop! Zooo-oo-oo! Bang!

That was the noise the rockets made all round Klip-Klap. They made such loud explosions that he jumped as high as a jumping squib in fright. They rushed up into the air and made holes in the little shed. Nothing could stop them. Away they went, shooting up high, and then bursting into clouds of little coloured stars.

Klip-Klap was so frightened that he really didn't know what to do; so he did a very silly thing. He took hold of the biggest rocket of all and clung to it. Then suddenly another box of coloured matches flared nearby and set light to the rocket.

Whoo-ooo-ooo-whiz-splutter-bang! The rocket shot up into the air with Klip-Klap hanging on to it for dear life. He was too surprised to let go. Up he went and up and up and up. It seemed as if that big rocket was never going to stop.

Higher and higher it went, till it reached the clouds. Klip-Klap saw the moon behind them, and wondered if the rocket would land there.

But, of course, it didn't! It suddenly came to a stop in mid-air, and burst into hundreds of coloured stars. Klip-Klap saw them, and shivered with fright.

Then he began falling with the rocket-stick. Down he went and down and down. He turned over and over as he fell, and he groaned loudly.

"I wish I hadn't been inquisitive! I wish I hadn't meddled! I wish I was a nice little gnome like all the rest! I wish – I wish!"

Down he went and down, till – *plop!* he fell into a pond – and would you believe it, it was the very pond that Quick-Eye the chief gnome had put in

his garden for his goldfish!

Wasn't it a strange thing? It shows what a long way the rocket had travelled in its flight through the air.

Splash! In went the gnome, up to his eyes in water. The goldfish swam away in terror. Quick-Eye came running out to see whatever the matter was.

"Good gracious me!" he cried in surprise, when he saw the dripping, frightened, sad and sorrowful Klip-Klap

crawling out of the water. "Can it be you, Klip-Klap? I thought I had told you to go right away from here?"

With tears and groans Klip-Klap told of his adventures with Peter Penny's fireworks.

"I've learned my lesson," he wept, making his face even wetter than it already was. "I'll never be meddlesome again, never, really I won't, Quick-Eye. Forgive me all my naughtiness, please do. I'll be good now, really I will."

Well, nobody could help being sorry for the poor little wet gnome at that moment, and Quick-Eye couldn't be angry with him any longer. He squeezed out his wet clothes for him, and then took him indoors to dry him by a big fire.

"I'll forgive you this once," he said, "because really you are a poor little unhappy thing now. But mind, Klip-Klap, I'll be very severe with you if you start getting into meddlesome habits again!"

Klip-Klap went home comforted. How good it was to put his key into the lock of his little front door once more! How lovely it was to see his old clock tick-tocking away in the corner! How nice it was to see his cosy bed waiting to be slept in!

"Horrid old fireworks!" he said, as he crept into his warm bed. "Whatever do boys and girls buy such nasty things for? Poor Peter Penny! He will be wondering what has happened to his store of fireworks! I will send him a big box of gnome-chocolates to make up."

He did – and Peter Penny was so surprised and delighted that he quite forgot to grieve for the loss of all his fine fireworks. As for Klip-Klap, he certainly learned his lesson, for never again did he meddle with anything that wasn't really and truly his own business!

Hooray for
Shuffle the Shoemaker!

"Do you know who's taken the cottage at the corner of the green?" said little Button, popping his head round Shuffle's kitchen door.

"No, who?" asked Shuffle, pricking up his pointed ears.

"Mr Pah!" said Button. "And all I can say is I'm very glad I don't live in Tiptop Village! I couldn't bear to have Mr Pah poking his nose into my affairs, and saying 'Pah!' to this and 'Pah!' to that."

Ma Shuffle looked dismayed. "Of all the people we could do without in this village, Mr Pah is the one!" she said. "I've met him before. He'll look in here and see what little Shuffle's doing, and he'll say 'Pah! What an old-fashioned way to mend shoes!' And he'll look into my cupboard of spells and say 'Pah! Is that the best you have? What a poor lot!' He just takes the heart out of you, that magician."

"Oooh, is he a magician?" said little Button.

"Yes, and a rich one, too," said Ma. "He's often offered a sack of gold pieces to anyone who knows better than he does, but nobody's ever won it yet!"

"Oooh," said Button again, and he looked at little Shuffle. "A sack of gold, Shuffle! I wish we had that!"

"Well, you'll never get it, Button, so forget it," said Ma. "Now here's the parcel for your mother. Get along with it, and keep out of Mr Pah's way if you can!"

Mr Pah was certainly a tiresome fellow. He looked in at Dame Scary when she was washing, and said, "Pah! If that's the way you wash, I shan't ask you to do my things for me!"

He poked his nose in at Mr Clang the blacksmith's, too. "Pah!" he said. "What stupid little bellows you use to blow up your fire, no wonder it

takes you ages to get it red-hot."

"Pah!" he said to Ma Shuffle. "What a collection of old-fashioned spells you have! Haven't you ever heard of the new ones?"

"I'd like to know a spell that would stop people poking their noses in where they're not wanted," said Ma, in a dangerous kind of voice.

"Pah! That's easy," said the magician. "You just take a pinch of pepper, a sprinkle of—" And then he caught the glint in Ma's eye, and thought better of it.

He backed out of the door. "I might tell you another day," he said.

"Yes, you do," said Ma. "I could use a spell like that straightaway!"

Well Mr Pah was so annoying that he really upset everyone in the village. "Can't we get rid of him?" they said to one another.

"He's so clever," said Dame Scary dolefully. "There's no getting the better of him."

Button and Shuffle put their heads together. "Listen, Button," said little Shuffle. "I've thought of a trick or two, not magic, you understand, because I wouldn't know better magic than Mr Pah. But just a trick or two."

"I'll help," said Button eagerly.

"Well, all you've got to do is to spread the news about that the wonderful enchanter, Mr Tricky, is visiting Tiptop Village, and giving a show," said Shuffle. "Tuesday afternoon at half past three. Tell everyone to be there. Mr Pah will hear about it, too, and he'll be along."

"But Shuffle, what's the trick you

know?" asked Button anxiously. "You'll have to be careful. If the trick doesn't come off, you'll get into trouble!"

"Yes, I know. But I'll have to risk that," said Shuffle. "They're silly tricks I've thought of, really, but that's just why I think they'll take Mr Pah in. Now you go off and spread the news about Mr Tricky, Button!"

Well, everyone soon heard that the wonderful enchanter Mr Tricky, was coming next Tuesday, and, of course, Mr Pah heard it, too.

"Ha! A chance to show him up!" thought Mr Pah. "A chance to show how much cleverer I am than this Mr Tricky, whoever he is!"

Everyone was on the village green at half past three. Shuffle was there, too, dressed in a flowing cloak and a pointed hat. He had rubbed a whisker spell on his face, so he had a very big beard, and didn't look at all like little Shuffle!

Mr Pah came, too, pahing and poohing as usual. He pushed his way to the

front. "I'm Mr Pah, the famous magician," he said. "I've never heard of you! There's nothing you can do that I can't. What are you going to do? What's that blackboard for?"

"I was going to teach a few spells," said little Shuffle, and he wrote down a few simple ones on the board. Mr Pah laughed till he cried.

"Sort of thing I learned in my pram!" he said. "You'll be teaching us that two and two make four next."

"Well, I wasn't going to teach that, I was going to show that six and four can make eleven, not ten," said Shuffle, his beard waving in the wind. "Can you do that, Mr Pah?"

There was a silence, as everyone listened for Mr Pah's answer.

"Impossible, and you know it," said Mr Pah. "No matter how you try, six and four will only make ten, not eleven. You're a silly fellow, Mr Tricky. I'll give you a sack of gold if you can make six and four into eleven!"

"Then watch me!" cried little Shuffle,

103

and everyone craned to see what he was putting on the blackboard.

"Now look, what's this?" asked Shuffle, and he wrote down "VI".

"Six!" cried everyone.

"And what's this?" asked Shuffle, and wrote down "IV".

"Four!" yelled everybody.

"Now watch me make six and four into eleven!" shouted Shuffle. "Here's my VI again – six as anyone can see – but I'm going to write my VI upside down this time – like this – ΛI – and I'll write it touching the VI – there you are – it's now XI – and isn't that eleven?"

"Yes, it is, it is!" shouted everyone in delight. Mr Pah stared in disgust.

"A trick, that's all," he said.

"I never said it wasn't," said Shuffle. "That sack of gold is mine, Mr Pah! And now another challenge, can you write a word that exactly describes you, and which reads the same upside down?"

"Impossible," said Mr Pah grumpily. "Never heard of one in my life!"

"Well, I learned it at school!" said little

Shuffle, and on the blackboard in very
large letters he wrote this word:

chump

"Chump!" gasped everyone. And they
laughed and laughed. Mr Pah turned

scarlet. He glared at little Shuffle, who was now solemnly turning the board the other way up. And lo and behold the word was exactly the same upside down. You try it!

Mr Pah stalked off, caught the next bus and never came back again. But he was honest enough to leave two sacks of gold pieces behind!

"You're rich, little Shuffle!" said everyone. "You're a prince! You can build a castle, and call yourself Prince Shuffle."

"I'm sharing out the gold with everyone in the village," said little Shuffle. "I'm no prince. I'm a village cobbler, and I'm happy in my job. Come along and help me count out the money, and this time six and four will make ten, and not eleven. No tricks this time!"

So he shared out all the money, and I'm really not surprised to know that when people meet him, they call out: "Hello, Prince Shuffle!" Are you?

The Girl Who Told Tales

Once upon a time there was a little girl who told tales. Her name was Minnie, and nobody really liked her. She was always running to her mother or to her teacher and telling tales about the other boys and girls.

"Mummy!" she would say, "do you know, Billy Brown put his tongue out at me!"

Or she would go to her teacher and say, "Oh, Teacher, Mary Jones cheated over her sums today. And I heard Mollie talking when she ought to have been quiet."

The teacher was always cross with her when she told tales.

"Leave me to find out these things for myself, Minnie," she would say. "Don't tell tales. It is a nasty habit."

But Minnie didn't stop, so none of the other boys and girls liked her at all. They could have told plenty of tales about Minnie if they had liked – for she was not a very good little girl herself. But they hated tales, and never said anything to their teacher or to their mother when Minnie took a pencil that didn't belong to her, or smacked them when they were playing with her.

One day, when Minnie was coming home from school, she saw a small boy making a bonfire in a field. She watched him, and then, hearing footsteps coming along by the hedge, she looked to see if it was the farmer coming along. It wasn't but she thought it was.

"Oh, please," she said, "there's a naughty little boy in that field, and he's making a bonfire."

The little man she spoke to stared at Minnie, and then looked at the small boy enjoying himself.

"Have you lost yourself?" asked the little man, who, now that Minnie came to

look at him closely, seemed rather
peculiar looking. He wore a pointed hat
with a long feather in it, and a tunic that
came down to his knees and was belted
with what looked like gold. Minnie stared
at him, and he asked her his question
again. "Have you lost yourself, I said?"

"What do you mean, lost myself?"
asked Minnie, in surprise.

"Well, don't you come from the Land
of Talebearers?" asked the little man,
sharply.

"No, I don't," said Minnie, beginning
to feel frightened. "I live in the village
here."

"Oh, no, you must be making a mistake," said the little man, taking hold of her hand. "Come along, I'll take you back home to the land you really come from."

Minnie struggled to get away, but to her enormous surprise everything around her disappeared and she found herself in what seemed a silvery mist that rushed by her. In a little while it cleared away and Minnie blinked and looked round. She was in a small village, with tiny, crooked houses here and there. Little creatures with thin, unkind faces were running about on spindly legs. They had high, sharp voices and Minnie didn't like the look of them at all.

The little folk ran up to see Minnie. "Who is she?" they cried.

"I found her in the wrong village," said the man in the feathered hat. "I thought she must be lost so I brought her here where she belongs. Give her a house and look after her."

"But I don't belong here!" cried Minnie, looking round at the man who spoke – but he had vanished! It was all very strange indeed. Minnie didn't like it. She stared at the sharp-faced little creatures round her and didn't like them either.

"We'll give you a nice house!" they cried. "Come on. You shall live with us in the Land of Talebearers."

Minnie was taken to a small, crooked house not far from where she stood. It had two little rooms in it, one a kitchen and one a bedroom.

"We all have the same," said a Talebearer called Snoop. "Keep your house clean, and come to join us for all meals except supper, which you cook for yourself."

Well, Minnie had to put up with it. It was no use running away because she didn't know where to run to. She didn't like being in that horrid little village at all. She found that she was expected to sweep, mop and dust her house, to light her own fire, and to cook her own supper. She also had to wash her own clothes. All meals but supper were eaten together out of doors, and the little folk took turns at helping to get them.

The head of the village was Higgle, the only round-faced man in the village. He gave the punishments – the scoldings and spankings – and he gave the rewards too for good work. These were chocolates and nice clothes.

Minnie knew how her own mother kept house, so she hadn't very much difficulty in keeping her tiny house clean. For a few days she swept and dusted very well – and then one morning she got up late, and heard the breakfast bell ringing before she had finished sweeping her rooms properly. So she hurriedly swept the dust under a mat and left it there. Then out she went to have breakfast.

"Do you know what I saw Minnie doing this morning?" a Talebearer said suddenly across the table. "I saw her sweeping all her dust under the mat! Dirty little girl!"

"Ooh, how lazy!" cried everyone, and stared at Minnie with round eyes.

Minnie went red and stared angrily all round her. She didn't say anything, but she thought a lot. Nasty little things!

The next day Minnie couldn't find a clean handkerchief, so she tucked a dirty one in her pocket, meaning to wash her others as soon as she could. But a little end hung out and Snoop saw it. He pulled it out of her pocket and showed it to everyone.

"Look! This is Minnie's handkerchief. Isn't she a dirty little girl! Fancy not having a clean handkerchief each day!"

"Ooh!" cried everyone, in disgust. Then Minnie lost her temper and slapped Snoop hard.

"You nasty taleteller!" she cried. "I hadn't a clean hanky this morning for the first time, and I meant to wash them all today. What do you want to pull it out of my pocket for?"

"She slapped me, she slapped me!" wept Snoop, holding his cheek. "I shall go and tell Higgle."

He ran off to Higgle's house, and Minnie heard him wailing there. She

114

went to her own house, feeling rather frightened. Soon Higgle came stalking up to her door and knocked on it.

"Snoop says you slapped him," he said sternly.

"Yes, I did," said Minnie, "and he deserved it."

"So do you," said Higgle at once, and before she could say anything more Minnie had a sharp slap too! That did surprise her. She burst into tears, slammed her door and flung herself down on her bed. What a horrid, horrid place this was!

After that Minnie was very careful to have a clean handkerchief each day, and never to sweep her dust under the mat. But will you believe it, those little Talebearers soon found things to say about her again!

"Do you know, Minnie's got a hole at the back of her sock!" she heard one whisper to another, and then pointed at her.

"Why didn't you tell me instead of him?" cried Minnie. "I didn't know I had one, and I could have gone home and mended it."

She mended the hole at once, quite determined not to do anything that would give the Talebearers anything at all to say about her. She knew that Saturday was near, when Higgle dealt out rewards and punishments – and Minnie was very anxious to have a box of chocolates and perhaps a smart pair of shoes with silver buckles like those some of the others were wearing.

She had kept her house beautifully for days. She had done everything she could.

She had been polite to the Talebearers, though not friendly, for she really didn't like them at all.

At last Saturday came, and everyone lined up in front of Higgle, who was wearing a very grand suit, with buttons of gold all over it.

Most of the Talebearers seemed to have good reports that week, and one after another went up to receive boxes of chocolates or to choose a hat with a feather in it or a pretty, coloured scarf. One or two had smackings and went off crying. Minnie longed for her turn to come, for there was a pair of shoes there that she wanted very much indeed. They were just her size, and had bright silver buckles and silver heels. They were really lovely.

"Now, Minnie," said Higgle. "Have you been good this week and done everything you should?"

"Yes, I think so," said Minnie, her eyes on the pretty shoes.

"Please, Higgle, I saw her yawning without putting her hand over her

mouth," a little Talebearer suddenly cried.

"And I saw her with a button off her dress!" called Snoop.

"And do you know, Higgle, when it was her turn to do the washing up on Wednesday she left a bit of mustard on one plate!" cried another.

"And she didn't turn her mattress yesterday when she made her bed!" said another, called Pry, because he was always peeping around.

"How do you know that?" cried Minnie, angrily. "You must have been peeping in at the keyhole as usual, you nasty, prying little thing. Higgle, he's always peeping to see what he can find out. He should be punished, not me."

"Well, there isn't really much to choose between you," said Higgle. "He says something nasty about you, and you say something nasty about him. You are both Talebearers, I can see. Come here, Pry, and you shall be spanked for peeping. As for you, Minnie, you can go to your house and put yourself to bed. Nobody seems to have a good word for you."

"Why do you listen to all those nasty tales?" shouted Minnie, losing her temper. "My mother and my teacher never listened to tales. They said that no nice person ever did pay attention to tales."

"Then why did you tell tales so often?" said Higgle, looking at Minnie with his strange yellow eyes. "I have been told that you were a real Talebearer and would be happy here."

"How can I be happy here with everyone saying nasty things about me?" said Minnie, crying.

"But you tell tales about others," said Higgle, puzzled. "Why shouldn't they tell tales about you? A little girl like you who loves to say nasty things about her friends should be very happy here with people just like herself."

"Well, I'm not happy," said Minnie, wiping her eyes. "I want to go back home."

"Oh, no," said Higgle, at once. "You can't go back home when you belong here. Taletellers must live with taletellers, otherwise it isn't fair. When you were at home you told tales about children who were much too nice to tell tales about you. So you had things all your own way, and it wasn't right. But here it is all quite fair – you all tell tales about one another. Now stop crying and do as you are told. Go and put yourself to bed for the rest of the day."

Minnie went. She cried bitterly when she was in bed, because she really was very unhappy and longed to go home. "I would never have told a single tale about anyone if I'd known there was a land for taletellers," she thought to herself. "How mean it was of Snoop and Pry to tell tales of me this morning – and I suppose it used to be just as mean of me to tell tales of the other boys and girls when I was at home. But they were nice to me and never said anything horrid about me to my teacher. No wonder they didn't like me! I must have been a nasty little girl. Perhaps I still am."

The next day Minnie got up, full of a new idea she thought of. Suppose she went to all the Talebearers and made a bargain with them? Suppose she said to them that if they promised never to tell tales of her she would never tell tales of them? Then things would be much happier.

Everyone agreed to her plan and nodded their mean little heads. Minnie was pleased. Now perhaps she would get a box of chocolates and those pretty shoes

the next Saturday. As no one was going to tell tales of her she didn't very much bother about her work that week, and her little house was dirty and badly kept. But Minnie didn't care. Higgle wouldn't know because he wouldn't be told!

When Saturday came they all went to him and stood in a line. One after another was praised and given a present, for no one told a single tale. At last it was Minnie's turn. She went up to get her chocolates, but suddenly Snoop cried: "She doesn't deserve chocolates, Higgle! Her house is as dirty as can be!"

"And she hasn't made her bed properly for a week!" cried Pry.

"And she spilt some ink all down the wall!" cried another.

Minnie turned and faced them in rage and disgust.

"You promised not to tell tales of me if I didn't tell them of you!" she cried.

"We know that," said Snoop, "but we thought you'd be good, and you haven't been. So it is our duty to tell Higgle about you."

"It isn't, it isn't!" cried Minnie. "Oh, you horrid creatures! You like telling tales so much that you even break your promises! All right, Higgle, punish me if you like. I have been lazy and bad this week, but please let me tell you all the things I have done, and don't listen to tales about me. I would rather tell you myself, and I will tell you truly."

"Wouldn't you like to tell a few tales about Snoop to pay him out for breaking his promise?" asked Higgle.

"No, I wouldn't," said Minnie. "I am not going to break my promise just

because he has broken his. He has been mean and nasty, but that's no reason why I should make myself the same, I shan't break my promise and I shan't tell tales. So there!"

Minnie was sent to her house again and had to stay indoors for two days as a punishment for keeping it so badly the week before. All that week she worked hard. She felt sure that all the Talebearers would find something horrid to say about her, but she didn't care. Let them! They were mean and horrid creatures and they could tell all they liked. She wasn't going to take any notice of them or what they did and she wasn't going to say anything about them, good or bad.

So all that week Minnie did her work well, and was quite polite to the Talebearers.

When Saturday came she took her place in the line as usual. She had quite made up her mind that she would never get any chocolates or the buckled shoes.

The Talebearers were angry with Minnie for doing her work so well that they had no tales to tell! So they decided to make up some tales about her. That would be fun!

So when Minnie's turn came you should have heard the tales they told! They were all quite untrue, and Minnie knew they were. She was surprised and hurt to hear what the little creatures said, and she went very red. But she said nothing at all.

"Minnie broke a plate the other day," said Snoop. It was quite untrue – she hadn't.

"Minnie was rude to me on Wednesday," said Pry.

"Minnie took one of my sweets when I wasn't looking," said another.

"Dear me!" said Higgle, looking grave. "What have you to say to these things, Minne?"

"Nothing," said Minnie. "None of them is true. That's the worst of Talebearers – when they find no tale they can tell, they make one up!"

128

"Have you any tales to tell about them?" asked Higgle.

"None at all," said Minnie, firmly. "I shall never, never tell another tale all my life long! I wish I never had told one. I didn't know till I came here what a horrid thing it was to tell tales about others – but now that I see what nasty creatures it makes people I've made up my mind I'll stop telling tales, no matter what other people say about me!"

"Dear me!" said Higgle again, looking at Minnie in a very curious way. "It seems to me, Minnie, that you don't belong here at all."

"I did at first," said Minnie, very red. "I

was nearly as bad as the rest of the Talebearers. But I don't belong now. You can keep me here if you like, but you won't ever hear me telling a tale!"

"You can't stay in the Land of Talebearers if you don't belong," said the Talebearers, all together. "We don't want you! You don't tell tales any more. Go away!"

"I'd like to," said Minnie, and she looked at Higgle. He took up a big box of chocolates, and the pretty pair of buckled shoes and gravely gave them to the little

girl. "You deserve them now," he said. "You have learned a big lesson. You may go back home – but if you should ever feel that you want to tell tales again, we shall be very pleased to see you here and to give you another little house."

Minnie took the chocolates and the shoes in delight. "Thank you," she said. "But you needn't ever expect me to come back again, Higgle. I never shall!"

"You must wait until the man who brought you comes here again," said Higgle. "He will take you home. I expect him today. He is bringing two little boys to live here."

"Oh, poor things!" thought Minnie. "I wish I could just tell them what to do to get away!"

In a short while the man with the feathered hat arrived, bringing with him two small boys. They were pleased to see Minnie and ran up to her. "Do tell us about this land," they begged.

"I haven't time," said Minnie, taking the hand that the man with the feathered hat held out to her. "But just remember this and it will help you – don't tell tales if you want to be happy!"

"But it's sometimes our duty to," said one of the boys.

"It's nobody's duty to tell tales," cried Minnie, and as she spoke she heard her own voice going fainter and fainter. The village of the Talebearers vanished and a silvery mist shone round her. When it cleared the little man was no longer there, and the fields she knew so well were around her. In one nearby was a little boy lighting a bonfire. Minnie stared in surprise.

"Why, did I dream all that?" she wondered. "When I went away that little boy was lighting his fire in the same place. Well, fairy time is different from ours, so I suppose I've come back to the same place and the same time as when I went away. How strange."

She stared at the small boy and his fire. But do you know, she never even thought of telling a tale about it! It was none of her business. She ran home, and her mother was delighted to see a

pleasant face, and to hear no tales at all. What could have happened to change Minnie?

For she was changed! Now she is a kindly, pleasant little girl, liked and trusted by everyone, very glad that she did not have to live for always in the Land of Talebearers. I hope I never go there, don't you?

You'd Better Be Careful, Stamp-About

It all began one morning when Mr Stamp-About took a walk down Bramble Lane. He wasn't in a very good temper, because his egg had been bad at breakfast-time, and he stamped along, frowning and grumbling to himself.

"I don't know what hens are coming to! Laying bad eggs! And to think I took such a big spoonful, too! Ugh!"

He came to Dame Kindly's cottage, and as he passed by her hedge, a spray of wild rose swung in the wind and scratched his cheek. Mr Stamp-About was very angry indeed.

"What! You'd lash out at me, and scratch me like a cat!" he shouted, and he hit out at the wild rose-bush with his stick. But the rose-bush only swung back again and scratched his ear.

Mr Stamp-About marched into the little garden and glared at the bush, which was covered with lovely roses. He saw a spade lying not far off and snatched it up. In no time he had dug up the wild rose-bush.

"There! That'll teach you to scratch people coming down the lane!" he shouted, and he stamped on the rose-bush, which was now lying on the ground.

Dame Kindly couldn't believe her eyes when she looked out of her window. She knocked loudly on the pane. "What are you doing? How dare you?"

Then Mr Stamp-About caught sight of three plump hens pecking about nearby, and he roared at them. "Are you hens laying bad eggs? Was it one of you who laid the egg I had for breakfast? Well, let me tell you I won't put up with it! Shoo! Go into your hen-house and sit down and lay good eggs. Shoo!"

And he waved his stick at the frightened hens and sent them scurrying away in fright. One fled out of the garden gate, squawking, and Dame Kindly came hurrying out of her door.

"Stop that! Stamp-About, how dare you chase my hens? Now one has fled away and I don't expect I'll ever get her back. And just look at my favourite wild rose-bush!"

"Pah! You've no right to have a bush that lashes out and scratches people," said Mr Stamp-About, most unreasonably. "As for the hens, I was only telling

yours what I think about birds that lay bad eggs. I had one for breakfast, and it tasted so—"

"Stamp-About, get out of my garden, and stop talking silly nonsense!" said Dame Kindly. "If you don't, I'll tell my husband to come and chase you out just as you chased my hens!"

Stamp-About gave such a loud laugh that the cat nearby fled away and hid in fright. "What! Tell your husband to chase me? That silly little man, who hardly comes up to my waist? You tell him I'll come and give him one good smack – and down he'll go, bump!"

Then out of the gate he went and gave it such a slam that the latch broke at once. Dame Kindly stared after him with angry tears in her eyes. To think that anyone should speak to her like that!

Someone called to her over the fence. It was little Long-Beard the brownie.

"Don't you take any notice of him, Dame Kindly. He's a loud-voiced bully. Just you send him in a bill for a new rose-bush, and if your hen doesn't come

138

back, tell him to pay for a new one. You get your husband to do that for you!"

"I will!" said Dame Kindly. So when her husband came home from work she told him all about Stamp-About's doings. The little man listened and frowned.

"Oh dear! I wish I was a great big fellow and could go after him! But he's so enormous and I'm so small, and he knows it. Still – I'll certainly send him in a bill if our hen doesn't come back."

So when the hen didn't appear that day or the next, he made out a bill.

To Mr Stamp-About.
Bill for
One rose-bush,
    pulled up in a temper   *£2*
One hen,
    driven away in a temper   *£5*
One gate latch,
    broken in a temper   *£3*
Upsetting my wife   *£10*
     £20

Payable to Mr Kindly AT ONCE.

Well, when Stamp-About got this bill he couldn't believe his eyes. Good gracious, what a temper he flew into! He stamped about his kitchen, shouting and yelling, till his next-door neighbour wondered if he had gone mad. He came peeping in at the window to see.

Stamp-About saw him, and called him in. "Hey, Mr Snoopy, come and see the bill that Mr Kindly has had the cheek to send in to me. What would you do if he had sent it to you?"

"Oh," said Snoopy, slyly. "I'd fight him, Mr Stamp-About. Biff, like this! Smack,

like that!" And he hit out at the air in front of him gleefully. "Down he'd go – and you could demand money from him then for insulting you by sending in such a rude bill!"

"That's a good idea of yours," said Stamp-About. "A very very good idea. I'll send him a letter to say I'll be along tomorrow morning at ten o'clock to give him a hiding. Aha! He's such a tiny fellow, I can shake him to bits if I want to, and then throw him into his duck-pond!"

So he wrote a letter to Mr Kindly, and

141

sent Mr Snoopy with it. Mrs Kindly opened it, because her husband was at work, and she sobbed bitterly when she read it.

"How unkind! What would my little husband do against a man like Stamp-About? I've a good mind to go and buy a grow-big spell from Witch Long-Nose, and make my husband drink it. Then he could beat Stamp-About – and serve him right!"

Snoopy hurried back to tell Stamp-About this. "Oh – so she thinks she can play a trick like that on me, does she?" he shouted. "Well – I'll be there at nine o'clock, instead of ten, before he's drunk any spell at all."

Now it happened that Snoopy met Long-Beard the brownie that morning, and he told him how Stamp-About was going to fight little Mr Kindly – and that he was going to be at his house at nine o'clock, instead of ten, so that Mr Kindly wouldn't have had time to drink the grow-big spell. He laughed and laughed as he told Long-Beard about it, for

Snoopy was not a nice fellow at all – but Long-Beard was worried. He didn't want the nice, friendly Kindlys to be upset and hurt.

He hurried off to Witch Long-Nose, and out of his own money he bought two bottles of spells. One was labelled *Drink this and grow little* and one was labelled *Drink this and grow big*.

Long-Beard went to Mr and Mrs Kindly's cottage and knocked at the door. Soon he was telling them that Stamp-About meant to come at nine o'clock instead of ten, hoping that Mr Kindly hadn't yet drunk the spell.

"But now listen," said Long-Beard. "Don't drink the grow-big spell, Mr Kindly. It tastes horrible, and the growing-big is very painful, and you would look dreadful, and—"

"Well, I'm certainly not going to drink the grow-little spell!" said Kindly.

"I know. Watch what I'm going to do," said Long-Beard. He carefully took off the two labels from the bottles and stuck them on again – but on the wrong bottles!

"Now listen!" he said, as he pressed the Grow-Little label on to the bottle of Grow-Big. "At nine o'clock tomorrow morning, you and Mrs Kindly must come and hide in my house – but leave these bottles on the table. If I know anything of Stamp-About, as soon as he sees it he'll drink the grow-big spell – or

what he thinks is the grow-big spell –
and then, to his enormous surprise,
he'll find himself dwindling away to
the size of your cat!"

Mr Kindly roared with laughter.
"Long-Beard, you're too clever for
words!" he said. "Right. We'll do what
you say."

So just before nine o'clock the next
morning the two Kindlys went into Long-
Beard's cottage and hid there, peeping
out behind the curtain to watch for
Stamp-About. On their kitchen table
they had left the two bottles – the grow-
big spell labelled Grow-Little and the
grow-little spell labelled Grow-Big.

"And if old Stamp-About likes to steal one of them by drinking it, he's only got himself to blame!" chuckled Long-Beard.

Well, at exactly nine o'clock, along came Stamp-About, singing a rude song about Mr Kindly, and swinging a stout stick. He thundered on the front door, but nobody came.

So he went round to the back door and looked in at the kitchen window. Ha – what were those two bottles standing on the table? He pushed open the back door and went in to see.

"What! A grow-big spell! So old Kindly got one after all, and meant to drink it before I came! And a grow-little spell to force down my throat when he had defeated me because he had grown so big. Ha – he's made a very big mistake! I'll drink the grow-big spell!"

And with that he took out the cork, tipped up the bottle and drank the whole spell down! *Gulp-swallow-gulp!*

But, of course, it was the grow-little spell he had drunk! Stamp-About, who had been expecting to grow big and touch

the ceiling, found himself growing small. Smaller – smaller – smaller still! Whatever was happening?

He gave a howl of fright. Why, he was smaller than the table – his head didn't even reach the top! Now he was so small that he wouldn't be able even to sit on the stool!

Next door Mr and Mrs Kindly and Long-Beard were waiting to see what happened. All they heard was a small frightened howling, rather like a puppy whining.

"He's drunk it – he's drunk the grow-little spell, thinking it was the grow-big spell, just as we hoped!" said Kindly. "Come along – we'll go and see!"

Yes – he was right, of course. How the Kindlys and Long-Beard laughed to see such a very small Stamp-About, howling in fright, trying his best to climb up on to a chair.

"Well, little fellow – what about that fight with me?" said Mr Kindly.

"No! No, no, no!" whimpered Stamp-About, trying to hide under the stool. "Don't be a bully!"

Then who should come into the kitchen but Whiskers, Mrs Kindly's cat. As soon as she saw the tiny little Stamp-About she hissed – and sprang! Stamp-About was so scared that he ran straight out of the door. The cat went after him. How it chased him – first into

this corner, and then into that. What a dreadful time poor Stamp-About had!

"It'll eat me! Save me, save me!" he cried.

Mrs Kindly began to feel very sorry for him. "Hasn't he been punished enough?" she said.

"No," said Long-Beard. "Let him be chased for five minutes more! Then maybe he'll talk some sense."

So for another five minutes the tiny

Stamp-About was pounced on, and chased here and there – and then Kindly picked him up and looked at him.

"Listen," he said. "I'm not going to fight you – I left my cat to do that. But what about that bill of mine? Are you going to pay for that rose-bush and my hen?"

"Yes, oh, yes," wept Stamp-About. "Only let me go, I must get a grow-big spell from somewhere."

"Well, drink a little out of this Grow-Little bottle," said Kindly. "We changed the labels. This is the spell to make you grow big! But don't you forget to pay our bill, Stamp-About – or we'll tell everyone in the village how our cat chased you round our garden, and they'll laugh whenever they meet you."

"No – don't tell them, please don't," begged Stamp-About. "Let me have a drink of that other spell. I hope it's not as painful as this one is!"

He drank some of the spell that would make him grow big again – and suddenly shot up to his right size. He sat down in a chair and groaned.

"I feel peculiar. My head is spinning. Take me home!"

"I'll take him home," said Long-Beard. "But first of all, what about the money for that bill of Kindly's, Stamp-About?"

"Take it out of my pocket," groaned Stamp-About. "Take all you want. I feel ill. I want to go home. All these spells – they don't suit me!"

So Long-Beard took the money from Stamp-About's pocket, and gave it to Mr Kindly to pay his bill. Then he pulled him to his feet to take him home.

"You've had a jolly good lesson, Stamp-About," he said. "You behave yourself in future."

Well, I don't expect old Stamp-About really will alter his ways – but I do know this; whenever he passes the Kindlys' cottage, he runs like a hare if he sees their cat on the wall. And I'm not a bit surprised at that, are you?

The Little
Silver Hat

Once upon a time there was a fairy called Silver-Wings. As you can guess, she had wings of silver, and her dress shone like silver, too. She wore silvery shoes, and was the merriest little thing imaginable.

She badly wanted a silver cap, but she couldn't get one anywhere. She tried in all the hat-shops she knew, but not one of them had a silver cap.

"We don't make silver caps," everyone said. "They would be too expensive!"

So Silver-Wings had to go without a silver cap and she was very sad about it.

And then one day she found one! It was such a surprise. She had been watching a little girl sitting sewing among the buttercups, and thinking what a good little girl she was. The child

153

was making a dress for her doll and was doing it as carefully as she could. In and out flew her needle, in and out.

The church clock struck eleven, and the little girl put down her work. "Time for a break," she said, and she took three biscuits out of a bag. She began to munch them, and the fairy crept nearer to look at the dress that the little girl was making.

And there, just by the little girl's sewing, was a silver hat! It was tall and shiny and silvery, and it shone in the sun.

Silver-Wings snatched it up in joy. She tried it on her head and it fitted perfectly! She ran to the nearest pool and looked at herself. She was as pretty as a picture!

Joyfully she danced through the buttercups and daisies, showing her new silver hat to the beetles and the butterflies, the ladybirds and the bees. They thought it was simply lovely.

"It's just what you wanted!" said a butterfly.

"It does suit you!" hummed a bee.

154

"Wherever did you find it?" cried a beetle.

"In this field!" said the fairy. "Just by that little girl over there."

A bee flew over to have a look at the little girl. He flew back again. "There is something the matter with that little girl," he hummed. "She looks worried."

The fairy flew off to see what was the matter. The little girl was certainly looking worried. She was hunting all over the place for something.

"I can't possibly get on with my work unless I find it!" Silver-Wings heard her say. "Oh dear, oh dear, wherever can it have gone?"

The fairy was sorry to hear that the little girl had lost something she wanted. She suddenly flew down beside the child and spoke to her in her high little voice.

"Can I help you? What have you lost?"

"I've lost my thimble," said the little girl. "The thing I put on my finger to stop the end of the needle from hurting it when I stitch."

The little girl looked at the fairy as she spoke and then stared in surprise.

"What's the matter?" asked the fairy. "Do you like my new hat?"

"Well," said the little girl, "you may think it's a hat, Fairy – but I think it's my thimble!"

And so it was! The fairy had picked up the little girl's thimble and had taken it for a hat! Would you believe it!

They stared at one another. Then the little girl began to laugh. How she laughed!

"Fancy using my thimble for a hat!" she cried. "But oh, it does fit you so beautifully and you look so sweet in it! It's just what you wanted!"

"Yes, isn't it?" said the fairy, taking it off sadly. "I'm sorry I took it, though, and made you hunt for it. Here it is."

"Now listen, Fairy," said the little girl. "I will finish my doll's dress and use my thimble till lunch-time. Then I will go home – but I will give you my silver thimble for a hat! I have another thimble at home, so I can spare you this one!"

Wasn't it nice of her? The fairy sat beside the little girl for the rest of the morning and watched her sewing quickly

and neatly, with the silver thimble on her middle finger – and then, when the church clock struck one, the little girl folded up her work, and gave the fairy her thimble.

"There you are!" she said. "You may have it! Come and peep at me sometimes and let me see how nice you look in your thimble-hat!"

So now Silver-Wings has a silver hat – though, if ever you see her, you will know at once that it is only somebody's little thimble!

Tell-Tale
Tommy

Tommy was staying down at the seaside with his cousins. There was Jean, the eldest. Then Peter came next. He was Tommy's age. Then there was Bobby. So Tommy fitted in nicely.

His cousins were jolly, noisy children, who loved digging in the sands, paddling in the waves and hunting for shells and seaweed. They welcomed Tommy, and let him share all they did.

Sometimes they were naughty. Once Jean went round the edge of the cliff when the tide was coming in, and that was forbidden, because sometimes people got caught by the waves and couldn't get back.

Tommy was shocked. He ran to tell his Aunt Emily, who was Jean's mother.

"Jean disobeyed you," he said. "She went round the cliff when the tide was coming in."

So Jean was punished, but Aunt Emily was not very pleased with Tommy either. "You musn't tell tales," she said. Jean said that, too.

"You're mean. You told tales about me and got me punished," she said. "You're a nasty, mean, horrid boy!"

Tommy ran to Aunt Emily. "Jean called me a nasty, mean, horrid boy," he cried.

"Well, so you are if you keep coming and telling tales," said Aunt Emily sharply.

The next day Peter lost his temper with Bobby and kicked his sandcastle down. Bobby cried, and Tommy, who was watching, ran to Jean.

"Jean, come and tell Peter to behave himself. He's knocked down Bobby's castle."

"Tell-tale," said Jean at once. "Tell-tale. I expect Bobby was naughty and deserved it. Anyway, why come and tell me? If you want anything done about it you can do it yourself, tell-tale."

Tommy hated being called a tell-tale. But it's what he was, and each day he managed to tell some kind of tale about the others. Poor Bobby got smacked for wading into the sea with his shoes on, and he, too, was angry with Tommy.

"I could have dried them in the sun. You told tales about me and made Mummy smack me. Here's a jolly good smack for you, too."

And he gave Tommy a slap on his bare leg. Tommy yelled and ran crying to his aunt.

"Bobby smacked me. Look at the red mark on my leg."

"Tell-tale, tell-tale, tell-tale!" chanted the three listening children. "We don't like Tommy Tell-Tale, we don't like Tommy Tell-Tale!"

The next day Tommy went to sail his new ship. His father had sent it to him, and he was very proud of it. He showed it to the others. They thought it was lovely, too. It was not very big, but it was well-made and beautiful, with its little red sail and sturdy mast.

"She's called *Sea-Foam*," said Tommy. "I shall sail her today when the tide goes out. She will float beautifully on one of the pools. I'll give you each a turn at holding her string."

Sea-Foam did sail beautifully. She didn't fall over on her side at all, as most toy ships do. She sailed very straight and upright and her little red sail gleamed in the sunshine.

"Isn't she lovely! Doesn't she sail well!" cried Peter, dancing about round the pool. "I bet she could sail to France and back.

What a pity there aren't any waves on this pool. I bet *Sea-Foam* would sail beautifully over even big waves."

"There are quite big waves on the sea," said Jean. "Couldn't we take *Sea-Foam* there instead of this pool, and see her bob up and down?"

"Oh, yes," said Tommy, pleased. "We can hold on to the string tightly."

So they took *Sea-Foam* to the sea, and let her sail there. They waded out to above their knees, where the waves were quite big, but *Sea-Foam* didn't mind how bumpy they were; she bobbed over them as upright as ever.

"She's a good ship, a very good ship,"

said Bobby. "Let me have a turn at holding her now, Tommy."

But before Bobby could take the string a bigger wave than usual came, and it knocked Tommy right over. It was a good thing he had on his swimsuit, and it didn't matter his getting wet, but, oh dear, he let go of *Sea-Foam*'s string, and the little ship sped away on the waves.

"Quick, quick, get my ship," spluttered Tommy and Jean, Peter and Bobby began to wade after *Sea-Foam* as quickly as they could.

But the tide was going out, and the sea took *Sea-Foam* far away. There she bobbed, out of reach, for not one of the children could swim.

Tommy howled. So did Bobby. Jean felt the tears come into her eyes, too; and even Peter blinked. Such a lovely ship, and now she was gone, she was nothing but a tiny red speck on the deep-blue sea.

They were all sorry for Tommy. He ran to his Aunt Emily, crying bitterly. "My new ship's lost. The sea took her away. The others made me take her to the big waves instead of sailing her on the pool."

"Now, don't say unkind things," said Aunt Emily. "It was nobody's fault, really. I'm very sorry your new ship is gone."

Tommy went about with red eyes all day long. Whenever he thought of *Sea-Foam* he sniffed miserably. Jean, Peter and Bobby were very sorry for him.

"Come for a walk over to the farm

after tea," they said to Tommy. They knew he loved going to the farm. "We're going."

Tommy shook his head. "I don't want to go," he said. "I feel so unhappy that I don't want to do anything. I keep on and on thinking of *Sea-Foam* lost in the big waves out to sea. Perhaps she has sunk to the bottom now and is a wreck."

Jean went to her mother. "Mummy, do you think that instead of going to the farm, Peter and Bobby and I could go down to the beach and just see if Tommy's ship has been washed up? The tide's in now and sometimes it brings back things it took away, like one of my shoes that once got lost."

"Well, you know I don't like you on the beach with the tide in, because we get such sudden big waves," said her mother. "But today, just for once, you may go; but be careful of the waves now, and watch out for any big ones."

"We will, Mummy," said Jean, pleased. Their beach was often dangerous in a high tide, for the shore was steep. Still,

Jean was a sensible girl, and would look after herself and the others.

She went to tell Peter and Bobby. "We won't tell Tommy, because he'll be upset all over again if we don't find *Sea-Foam*," she said.

So they set off without Tommy. They went down to the beach, and began to hunt carefully along the high-water mark. They found an old shoe burst at the toe, some enormous fronds of ribbon seaweed, a broken spade, the handle of a bucket, a few old tins and a very big shell.

But they didn't find *Sea-Foam*. They turned back to hunt again, and Peter carefully scraped away at the piles of

seaweed. Then, quite suddenly, Bobby saw something red sticking out from beneath a little pile of shells and sea weed. He bent down and gave a yell.

"Look! Do look! Here's *Sea-Foam*! I saw her red sail."

The other two ran up, thrilled. Peter pulled the ship out carefully. Its mast was broken. Its red sail was torn. Some of the white paint had been scraped off by stones that it had been thrown against. But it was still *Sea-Foam*.

"I can dry and mend the red sail," said Jean happily.

"And I can easily make her a new mast," said Peter.

"And I've got a little tin of white paint, so I can paint the bare places on her," said Bobby. "Then she'll be quite perfect again. Won't Tommy be pleased!"

"We'll mend her before we tell him," said Jean. "Come on, let's go back now and do the mending. Then we can give the boat to him before he goes to bed."

Now, Tommy had been feeling lonely and sad after tea, and he had wished

that, after all, he had said he would go
with the others to the farm. He went to
the window and looked gloomily out over
the sea.

And, to his very great surprise, he saw
Jean, Peter and Bobby down on the
distant beach. He stared in astonishment.

"The bad, naughty children. They
know we aren't supposed to go on the
beach when the tide is high. They've
disobeyed Aunt Emily again. I'll tell her."

He went to find her, but he couldn't.
When he got back to the window he saw
that the three children had left the beach

and were going into the house, carrying something very carefully. He couldn't see what it was.

"They've found something on the beach, I suppose," said Tommy. "They'll come up and show me."

But they didn't. They went into the garden shed and shut the door. When Tommy went to it it was locked.

"Wait a bit. You can't come in yet. We've got a secret," yelled Peter.

"Beasts!" yelled back Tommy. "First, you go and disobey Aunt Emily. I saw you on the beach. And then you lock yourselves up and won't let me share. I hate you."

He rushed off before they could say anything. He went to find Aunt Emily, and at last found her in his uncle's study, sitting with his uncle.

"Uncle Ben, the others went down to the beach at high tide," began Tommy, in his usual tell-tale voice. "And they've come back and locked themselves into the shed, and won't let me share their secret. They're mean to me. They said

they were going to the farm, but they weren't. They told me a story. They went on the beach at high tide instead, and you said that anyone who did that would be sent to bed."

"So I did," said Uncle Ben, looking seriously at Tommy. "So I did. Ah, here come the others. We'll see what they've got to say."

Aunt Emily said nothing. She sat with her head bent over her sewing, only looking up when the others came in.

Peter carried *Sea-Foam* behind his back, and his eyes sparkled. He had put in a fine new mast. Jean had mended the hole in the red sail, Bobby had touched up the bare places with white paint. What a glorious surprise for Tommy.

Tommy gave them a horrid look. Then their father spoke. "Have you been down on the beach at high tide?"

"Yes," said all of them.

"Why?" asked their father.

"To try and find Tommy's lovely ship," said Jean. "Mummy said we might, just for once. And oh, we found it, Daddy; and we've mended her and painted her, and now Tommy can have her again."

Peter brought out the lovely little ship from behind his back. Tommy gave a gasp of joy and ran to take it. But his uncle stopped him.

"Wait," he said. "Tommy, you told tales about the others, didn't you? You tried to get them into trouble by telling us that they were on the beach at high tide, and all the time they were looking for your lost ship for you. You told me they had locked themselves in the shed and wouldn't let you share their secret, but all they were doing was mending

172

your ship and preparing a lovely surprise for you."

Jean, Peter and Bobby looked at Tommy in surprise and disgust.

"Tommy Tell-Tale," said Peter at once. "I've a good mind to throw your ship on the floor and stamp on it, but it's too beautiful for that. Tommy Tell-Tale!"

Tommy stood looking white and shocked. How awful to tell tales about the others when they had been trying to do something kind for him. How really terrible.

His uncle spoke sternly. "You are not to have your ship back, Tommy. You don't deserve it. The others shall have it."

Jean expected Tommy to burst into tears or stamp in a temper. But he didn't. He gave them all a great surprise.

"They can have my ship," he said, in a strange choky voice. "I'll give it to them for their kindness and because I'm dreadfully sorry I told tales. I'll never, never do such a thing again."

He rushed out of the room. Jean looked at her father. "Couldn't we all share the ship, Tommy too?" she said. "I think he's really sorry, Daddy, and maybe he won't tell tales any more now."

"Very well. Share it," said Daddy. "But Tommy's share goes the minute he tells another tale."

But Tommy still has a share in the beautiful little ship, so you know what that means. He isn't Tommy Tell-Tale any more. As for *Sea-Foam*, she sails as beautifully as ever, and has never been lost again.

The Forgotten Pets

Helen and Nick had a good many pets, but they didn't love them very much. They had a rabbit in a big hutch. They had a yellow canary in a cage. They had a dog and a nice kennel for it.

But not one of the pets was happy. "My hutch smells," said the rabbit. "It hasn't been cleaned out for days!"

"I haven't any water in my pot, in my pot, in my pot," trilled the canary. "Helen has forgotten again."

"I want some warm bedding in my kennel because the nights are cold," barked the dog.

But the children didn't look after their pets as they should, because they didn't love them. They shouldn't have had pets, of course, because they weren't the right kind of children for them.

One day the rabbit sent a message to a pixie friend of his: "Come and help me. I am unhappy. The children who own me don't look after me at all."

The pixie went to two or three of his friends and they made a plan.

The next day, when the two children were coming back from school, the pixies met them.

"Would you come and stay with us for

a day or two?" said Twinkle, the chief pixie. "We don't see many little boys and girls in Fairyland, and we would like to give you a little house to stay in, and we would be so glad if you would let all the fairies, pixies and brownies have a look at you."

The children thought this sounded lovely. "Yes," said Helen, "of course we'll come. Fancy having a little house of our own."

"You shall have plates and cups with your name on too," said Twinkle.

"How lovely!" said Nick. "We shall be just like pets."

"You will," said Twinkle. "We will look after you well, and not forget you at all."

They took the children to Fairyland. They showed them into a dear little house with two rooms. A good fire burned in one room, for it was cold. There were two beds in the bedroom, but they only had one blanket on each.

"We'll be cold with only one blanket," said Nick.

"Oh, we'll bring you more," said

Twinkle. "Now see, aren't these dear little cups and plates and dishes – all with your names on!"

They certainly were nice. The children were very pleased. They went into the garden of the little house. It was wired all around, and there was a gate, tall and strong, with a padlock on it.

"We'll lock you in, so that no bad brownie or pixie can get you," said Twinkle. "Now we'll just go and tell everyone you are here, and then they can come and look at you through the wire, and you can talk to them and tell them all your news."

The first day was great fun, and the meals were delicious, served in the cups and dishes with their names on. But when night came, and the children went into the little house, they found that it was very cold. The lovely warm fire had gone out and there was no coal or wood to be seen. And dear me, Twinkle had forgotten to bring the extra blankets for their beds!

They shivered. "We'll call for Twinkle,

178

or go and find him," said Helen. So they called. But nobody came. They tried to open the gate but it was locked. They went back to the cold house and hoped their little candle would last till the daylight came.

They were so cold that night, they couldn't sleep. The wind howled round. Helen was thirsty, but she couldn't find any taps in the house at all.

She felt cross with Twinkle. "I do think he might look after us better," she said.

"He promised to bring us warm blankets, and he didn't. And there isn't a drop of water to drink! After all, if he wants us to be like pets here, he ought to treat us well. We can't look after ourselves!"

The next day the children waited for Twinkle to come. He came at last – but he didn't bring them much breakfast.

"I'll bring you a better lunch," he said. "What's that – you want a drink? All right, I'll bring that later. I'm rather busy at the moment. And yes – I'll bring those blankets. How stupid of me to forget!"

But he didn't come again that day. Other pixies came and stared through the fence, but as the gate was locked they could not get in to give the children any food or water. They grew angry and frightened.

Twinkle came about six o'clock. "So sorry not to have been able to come before," he said. "I had such a lot to do. Oh dear – I've forgotten the water again – and the blankets. Still here is some bread and butter. I'll go back for the other things."

180

"Only bread and butter," said the poor children, who were now dreadfully hungry. "Oh dear! Bring us something else, please. And we think we'd like to go home tomorrow."

Twinkle went off. He didn't come back that night! Helen and Nick were so thirsty that they cried. They didn't undress because they were too cold. They sat huddled on the beds, feeling miserable.

"It's raining," said Helen. "Let's go out and open our mouths to the rain – then we shall get a drink."

They did, but they also got soaked through, which made them colder than ever. There was still no fire, because Twinkle had forgotten to bring them wood or coal. The candle had burned out. It was dark and horrid in the little house, which could have been so cosy and comfortable.

"I don't call this being pets!" sobbed Helen. "We're forgotten. They don't love us a bit – they don't remember to give us water or proper food, or to keep us warm. They don't deserve to have us as pets!"

Nick was quiet for a moment. Then he spoke in a serious voice. "Helen – I think the pixies have done this on purpose! This is how we keep our pets! We forget to give them proper food – we forget to give them fresh water – we don't clean out their cages when we should – and you know we didn't give poor old Rover any warm bedding in his kennel these cold nights."

"Oh," said Helen. "Oh, poor Rover! Nick, I know what it feels like now, don't you, to be in a cage, not able to look after

ourselves or get food – and then be
forgotten. It's dreadful. It's wrong. I'll
never do such a thing again. I'll always
love my pets and look after them."

As soon as she said that a strange thing
happened. She felt warm and cosy and
comfortable – and as she felt round, she
gave a loud cry.

"Nick! I'm not in that little house –
I'm in my own bed at home! How did it
happen?"

They never knew how it was that they had gone from Fairyland to their own beds, and I don't know either – all I know is that as soon as they had learned their lesson, they were back home again.

They didn't forget what they had felt like when they had been forgotten pets in Fairyland. They love their pets now, and care for them well. It was a good idea of Twinkle's, wasn't it, to make them into pets, and then pretend to forget them?

He Wouldn't
Go in the Water!

"Charlie, come and have a swim!" shouted Alan.

"Yes, do!" said Jenny. "It's so hot today."

Charlie was lying lazily on the rubber bed that his father and mother used on the beach. He shook his head.

"I don't want to swim," he said. "I'm too comfy."

"Don't be so lazy!" said Robert. "You haven't even paddled today!"

"The water's cold," said Charlie.

"But the sun is so hot, and it's lovely in the sea when the water is warm in the sun," said Lucy.

"I always think the water feels colder on a hot day than it does on a cold day," said Charlie, not moving. "I tell you, I'm not going in the water, and none of you can make me. So there!"

"Well, Charlie, do lend us that bed you're lying on," begged Jenny. "It's such fun to sit on it when we're in the sea. We have great fun pushing one another off."

"I'm not going in the sea and I'm not going to lend you my bed," said Charlie selfishly. "I'm going to lie here and snooze in the sun – and if anybody comes and annoys me I'll knock them down flat in the sand!"

That was just like Charlie! He was big, and if anybody wouldn't do what he said, he just pushed them over. He was selfish too, and wouldn't lend any of his things. The children ran off, grumbling. "It's too mean of Charlie," said Lucy. "He knows how we all love to play with that rubber bed. He's the only one of us that has one – and his mother said he could lend it to us when we swam."

"Oh, never mind!" said Robert. "What's the use of bothering about people like Charlie. He'll get his punishment one day. My mother says laziness and selfishness always bring their own reward."

They darted into the sea, jumping high over the little waves, and having a lovely time. The tide was coming in. The waves got bigger and longer, and suddenly one swept right up the sandy beach.

Lucy stopped and looked up the sand. "Oh," she said, "do look at Charlie! He's gone fast asleep on his rubber bed, and the sea has just reached him. Shall we wake him?"

"No," said Alan, with a giggle. "He wanted his sleep and he forbade anyone to disturb him. Let him be."

The waves touched the bed. One big one ran all round it. The next one lifted it up a little – and after that the bed was afloat!

"Oooh!" said Robert. "It's floating! Look at this wave – it'll take the bed back with it!"

It did – and the bed floated neatly down the beach. The tide turned again and took the bed with it. Away on the bobbing waves went the floating bed, carrying lazy Charlie with it.

The children felt frightened then. They didn't want the bed to float right away, so they shouted to Charlie. At the same moment a wave splashed over the bed and went on his face. He woke up with a jump.

"Who's throwing water at me?" he shouted. "I'll push you over, I'll . . ." And then Charlie saw where he was – no longer on the beach but bobbing on the waves.

"Come back before the water gets too deep!" yelled Robert. "Come on – get back at once!"

There was nothing for Charlie to do but to jump straight into the water in all his clothes and begin to walk back to the shore, dragging the bed with him. My goodness, the water felt cold! You see, Charlie had been lying in the hot sun and he was as warm as new-made toast, so the water felt terribly cold.

How the children giggled when they

saw Charlie wading back through the sea, up to his waist in the water, looking as angry as could be!

"You had to go in the water after all, Charlie!" called Lucy.

"You said nobody could make you go in the sea if you didn't want to – but you've had to all the same!" shouted Robert.

"Is the water nice and hot?" yelled Alan.

Charlie's face was black as thunder. He meant to punish all the children, but when he had got back to the shore, who should come down to the beach but his mother! How surprised and cross she was when she saw Charlie coming out of the sea with the rubber bed, dressed in his shorts and T-shirt!

"You very naughty boy!" she cried. "You've been swimming in your clothes – just because you were too lazy to change into your trunks, I suppose! Go straight home and dry yourself, and then go to bed."

"But, Mum—" began poor Charlie. But his mother wouldn't listen to a word.

She hustled him up the steps to the parade, and made him leave the rubber bed behind him on the beach.

"You don't deserve to have such a nice plaything," she scolded. "Leave it for the other children to play with. Go along home – and mind you're in bed when I come!"

So Charlie had to run home and go to bed on that lovely hot day, and the other children played with the rubber bed, and had great games with it.

"Serves him right, the lazy, selfish boy!" said Lucy. "Perhaps that will teach him a lesson."

It did! Charlie never sleeps on the rubber bed any more, even when the water really is cold. No – he's in his swimming-trunks before anyone else, and into the water he goes with a splash, to play with his friends.